Who are these Christians?

When the others had left the room, Mara turned her head slightly on the pillows so that she could better see her grandmother.

"They are kind people," she said.

Her grandmother glanced at the closed door. "They are that, but then they are Christians."

"Christians!"

Mara had heard tales of the Jews who had accepted a pagan religion. She remembered their being called Nazarenes, and although the group had been called "Christians" in a derogatory manner, they had chosen to keep the name that meant that they were "like Christ." It surprised her that her grandmother had spoken of them so fondly when she knew the truth. A cold shiver ran through Mara.

"We must leave!"

DARLENE MINDRUP is a full-time homemaker and homeschool teacher. A "radical feminist" turned "radical Christian," Darlene lives in Arizona with her husband and two children. She believes "romance is for everyone, not just the young and beautiful."

Books by Darlene Mindrup

Mark of Cain

Darlene Mindrup

Heartsong Presents

To my sister, Dorothy. You were a bratty kid, but you've turned out to be a pretty good friend. I love you!

A note from the author:
I love to hear from my readers! You may correspond with me by writing: **Darlene Mindrup**
Author Relations
PO Box 719
Uhrichsville, OH 44683

ISBN 1-57748-787-7

MARK OF CAIN

All of the characters and events in this book are fictitious. Any resemblance to actual persons, living or dead, or to actual events is purely coincidental.

Cover illustration by Dominick Saponaro.

PRINTED IN THE U.S.A.

one

Adonijah sighed with satisfaction as his glance swept quickly over the bright fields bursting forth with a vast crop of wheat. The proud feeling of ownership he felt surprised him, for he had only lived in this region six years. In actuality, the land was not his, but belonged to his friend Barak.

His brown eyes darkened with remembrance of the last time he had seen his home of Jotapata. Unknowingly, his hand went up to his bearded left cheek, and he absently rubbed the spot where his adopted uncle had slapped him so long ago. Although Uncle Simon had been furious with Barak for taking a foreign wife, his real anger came from his belief that Barak and Adonijah had forsaken the faith of their fathers. The memory of his uncle's rejection still left Adonijah feeling cold inside.

Having discovered that the man called Jesus was, in fact, the Messiah, Adonijah and Barak had tried to convince others, only to find themselves considered infidels and cast out by the Jewish community. Old Beker, who was an outcast himself, had warned them that this would be so.

Adonijah looked back at the fields where the reapers were already harvesting. Seating himself on a large rock, he pulled one leg up and wrapped his forearms lightly around it. His short brown tunic ruffled slightly in the cool spring breeze. Although his eyes continued to scan the field, his mind was elsewhere.

How had he, a proud Jew from a fine family, come to feel so at home in Samaria, of all places? Six years ago he would never have thought it possible, but now he felt again the thrill of proprietorship.

The gleaners moved along in the wake of the reapers, adding the refuse wheat to their baskets. Jewish law dictated that after an area had been harvested, the poor and the widows could follow behind and gather what the reapers had missed. Although as Christians he and Barak were no longer bound by the old laws, this was not a custom he wanted to give up. Besides, Jesus Himself had said that He had not come to abolish the law, but to fulfill it. Adonijah wished only that there was more that he could do for these people. It would take time, but they had already seen a beginning.

All over Palestine, Christian brethren were giving to a community pool, and then their donations were being distributed to those who were in need. Both he and Barak thought it a fine idea, as did the other believers here in Samaria, and slowly they were beginning to do the same.

He found himself studying one young woman as she gracefully migrated from area to area. He couldn't say exactly when he had first noticed her, but lately he found himself seeking her among the other gleaners. Although she was raggedly dressed, there was something almost alluring about her. It intrigued him that she steadfastly kept to herself.

Adonijah noticed others glance at her from time to time, their looks openly hostile. Growing curious, Adonijah lifted himself from the rock and began to slowly meander in her direction. He stopped periodically to speak to others, but his course never wavered.

Just as he was about to reach his destination, one of his workers called to him, causing him to stop in his tracks. The man hurried up, and Adonijah recognized him as one of the newer workers that Barak had hired the previous week.

"Master," he called again, panting with the exertion of running.

Adonijah waited for him to catch his breath and continue.

"Master, the south side of the field is complete. Where

shall I go next?"

Glancing past the man's shoulder, Adonijah could see that the southern field was stripped of grain. The other reapers had retreated, leaving only the gleaners still sifting among the fallen wheat. Smiling, he returned his attention to the man.

"Well done, Hermon."

Hermon smiled with pleasure as he awaited further instructions. The sun was lowering in the west and twilight would be soon upon them.

"The day is almost done," Adonijah told him. "Go ahead and present yourself to the foreman and collect your wages. You can start in the eastern field tomorrow with the others."

Bowing low, the other man hurried away. Adonijah watched him making his way down the slopes, shoulders erect as he swung along. A small smile tilted Adonijah's lips. If all the workers were as zealous as Hermon, the grain would be in the storehouses long before time. Although Hermon was of advancing years, his zest for work put the younger men to shame.

Turning back to continue to his destination, Adonijah was brought up short. The woman was gone.

≈

Mara dropped her bag on the small table just inside the door of the tiny mud hut she shared with her grandmother. Closing her eyes, she placed a trembling hand against her furrowed forehead. A moment longer, and she felt sure that the handsome young man who watched over Barak's fields would have reached her.

Her hand slid down to conceal the huge purple spot that covered most of the left side of her face. The mark of Cain, most people called it, and they steadfastly shied away from any close proximity with her.

She felt certain that the young giant would have reacted in open revulsion and would have ordered her from the property. This could not be, for she was the only means of support now for her grandmother and herself.

Although a tear trembled on the ends of her lashes, she refused to allow it passage. She gritted her teeth with determination. No! There had been too many tears already, and tears had never solved anything.

Going to the open door, she glared angrily at the dusky blue sky overhead. Only a healthy fear and respect kept her from shaking a fist at that great expanse.

"Mara?"

Mara turned swiftly at the feeble call and hurried across the room to the area at the back of the hut where her grandmother now spent most of her time. Since there was no money for oil, the sunlight from the open door was the only source of light in the murky darkness.

Moving gracefully around the few belongings cluttering the interior, Mara unerringly found where her grandmother patiently lay on an old straw mat.

Dropping to her grandmother's side, Mara stroked a hand lovingly across the wrinkled old forehead. "I am here, Grandmother."

Sighing, the old woman smiled slightly as Mara's cool hand continued to stroke her fevered brow. "You had a good day?" she inquired, her voice ending with a small croak.

Mara nodded, knowing that her grandmother probably couldn't see the movement in the dimness of the interior. "I had a good day. Now I must prepare you something to eat."

"I am not hungry," her grandmother refuted. "But I *would* like some water."

Smiling, Mara told her, "I will get it," but when she lifted the urn from the table, there was no water left. Biting her lip, Mara considered her options. They amounted to only two: Either she went to the well and got some more water, or her grandmother went thirsty.

Going back to the pallet, Mara dropped quickly to her

knees. "I must go for more water, Grandmother. Will you be all right until I return?"

Frowning, the old woman clutched Mara's hand. "You needn't go, Mara. I will be all right without the water."

Mara felt a lump rise to her throat. Always, her grandmother had cared for and protected her. It was Grandmother who held her while tears poured from a wounded heart after others had hurled abuse at her. Only Grandmother would understand what a tremendous chore it would be for Mara to go to the town well to retrieve water. Usually she waited until after darkness, knowing that she wouldn't meet any others, but Grandmother needed water *now*.

Pressing her lips tightly together, Mara rose to her feet. "I will return shortly."

Lifting the urn from the table, Mara hurried out the door, only to slow her steps as she reached the end of the path that joined the main road. Feet dragging, she forced herself to move onward.

The other huts around her reflected the poverty of those who lived within. There was little difference between the buildings except for the number of people going to and from each residence. This community had been set up by the residents of Sychar for those who were too destitute to afford land of their own.

When her parents had been alive, they had all lived together in Medeba, a small town just east of Jerusalem. Although she could remember little of those times, she *did* remember them as happy.

Then things began to change. A drought hit the land, and people and animals alike suffered. Before long, the people of the town started to look at Mara's family as the cause of their misfortunes. The mark of Cain, they said. In the end, her family had to move to another town. From then on they had been wandering pilgrims, never able to settle for very long at a time before some happening would be placed at their doorstep.

Using her veil to cover her face, Mara clutched the water pitcher tightly in her hand as she hurried to the well. Samaria was a land of plentiful water, and often families had their own springs feeding their lands, but not so in their little community. Instead, the women made the daily trek to the town's cistern. If only she could hole up inside their little hut and never have to face the world again. Before Grandmother had become ill, that was pretty much what she had done. But now it seemed Jehovah had other ideas.

Again she glared angrily at the sky overhead as she increased her steps. Still, it was better that this community had its own well and she didn't have to travel farther to Jacob's Well. There was no telling how many people she would have met along the way. She hadn't prayed to Jehovah for a very long time, but she found herself throwing up a hasty petition now. *Please, don't let anyone else be at the well.*

For once, Jehovah seemed to be showing her favor. Mara blew out her breath with relief when she realized that no other person was within sight of her destination. She quickly dropped the roped jar into the well, listening for the soft splash. Leaning her thighs against the cold stone, she pulled the heavy leather bucket up, bit by bit. Although she was small of stature, she was strong, and it took only a moment to fulfill her task. Gripping the urn tightly, she virtually ran back the way she had come.

Her grandmother lay as she had left her, still and silent, and for a moment Mara felt panic grip her. A slight sound must have reached the elderly woman, for her eyes slowly fluttered open. "Mara?"

Mara hadn't realized until that moment that she had been holding her breath. It rushed out of her at her grandmother's weak voice. "Yes, Grandmother. I am here."

Quickly pouring a cup of water, Mara dropped to her knees

and gently cradled her grandmother's gray head in her arm. Her grandmother drank thirstily, a soft sigh giving evidence of her relief.

"I am tired, Mara," she croaked. "I wish to sleep now."

As she laid her grandmother back against the mat, Mara's brow creased into a worried frown. It was so hard to leave her grandmother day in and day out, just to glean enough wheat each day for their meal the next day. Before her grandmother had become ill, it was she who gleaned in the fields and Mara who stayed at home grinding the previous day's forage into flour for their bread. Now, it was up to Mara to do both chores.

Still, she would gladly work her fingers to the bone and accept any abuse from anyone, if only her grandmother could be made well again. Each day saw her slipping farther and farther away, and Mara was beginning to think that death was imminent. As always, she wondered if it were true what the others said. Maybe it *was* her fault, all the bad things that seemed to plague them wherever they went. Maybe she was truly cursed.

First, Mara had been an only child. Then her mother had died from some unknown ailment, her father following shortly after when he had been trampled by an ox. Now, her grandmother might very well die, too.

Did the scriptures teach about such things? Since her father had been in her life such a short time, she had learned very little about the word of Jehovah, but she *had* been taught about the God of her people.

The tightness in her chest intensified. Going to the table, she pulled out the pestle and mortar and began to grind some of the grain that had been left from yesterday. With such intense feelings burdening her soul, it didn't take her long to grind the grain to a powdery mass.

Mixing the flour with a little water, she then moved outside the hut to the small oven that sat just inside a low garden wall. It wasn't until she had everything prepared that she noticed that the fire had gone out. Stifling an exclamation, she knelt quickly by the diminutive round structure and thrust her hands into the ashes. As she had feared, they were cold.

The tears that she had refused to allow now would not be stopped. Folding her arms against the oven rim, she dropped her head on them and sobbed quietly.

She was so tired, and her back ached horribly after gleaning all day in the hot sun. Now, there was no fire to prepare her meal. It would take too long to begin a new one, and she just couldn't bring herself to go to one of her neighbors and beg some fire from them.

Grandmother was too ill to tend the fire during the day, and Mara, as yet, was afraid to ask someone to come and look after her. She hadn't missed the unfriendly looks thrown her way during the last several days.

"Oh, Jehovah," she cried softly. "Why couldn't you let me die!"

Brushing angrily at the tears wending their way down her cheeks, Mara got slowly to her feet. There was nothing to be done now. Grandmother was too sick to eat, and Mara hadn't the heart.

Dragging herself back into the house, Mara placed her own sleeping mat next to her grandmother's so that she could be near her during the night. She felt the old woman shivering and moved closer to share her own body warmth. Although the days were sunny and fine for spring, the nights were still chilly.

Mara wrapped her arm and leg gently over her grandmother's shivering form since they had no blankets for covers. She felt the heat of her grandmother's fevered skin against her own. Tomorrow she must go for the healer. Since she had enough grain to last them through the next day, she could skip going to the fields to glean wheat. Getting Grandmother well was much more important. Surely the healer wouldn't deny them just because of Mara's disfigurement.

Although her mind was filled with tormenting doubts, her body was past endurance. She slept almost instantly.

※

Adonijah sat quietly at the table pulling his bread into little pieces. Anna and Barak exchanged glances, Barak shrugging wryly at Anna's questioning brow.

"Adonijah, is the food not to your liking?" Anna asked sweetly.

She was met with a blank stare. "What?"

Anna nodded at his plate, where his food had been heaped into little fragmented piles. Adonijah glanced down, sudden color filling his face.

"I am sorry, Anna. The food is fine." He pushed the plate to the side.

Barak leaned an arm against the table, his look focused intently on his friend's face. "Is there trouble, Adonijah?"

Adonijah hesitated before answering. "No. Nothing that need concern you. Just something that I noticed while surveying the wheat fields today."

Barak frowned at Adonijah's reluctance to continue. "Tell me."

Adonijah's glance swept briefly to Anna before returning to his friend. "There was a woman in the fields gleaning."

At Anna's sudden smirk, he scowled. "I knew you would think something like that," he told her huffily.

"Like what?" she asked, her eyes opened innocently wide.

Adonijah could see Barak trying to hide a grin behind his fingers as he stroked his lips. His scowl turned into a full glare. "It's not what you think. I only noticed her because the other gleaners seemed to be treating her rather. . .well. . .in a rather unfriendly manner."

Anna suddenly sobered. "That must have been Mara. I have heard of her from others. It seems that she has a disfigurement that the more superstitious see as the mark of Cain. They're afraid of her. They think she's evil."

Barak's voice rose slightly. "That's ridiculous. Have they harmed her in any way?"

Adonijah shrugged. "Physically, I don't know. Emotionally?" He shook his head, one dark eyebrow lifting upwards. "Only Jehovah knows."

Barak turned to his wife. "Do you know where she's from?"

"From what I understand, she and her grandmother moved here a few months ago. As far as I can tell, they have no family or friends here, so I'm not certain why they came."

Grunting, Adonijah reached for his goblet. "Perhaps it is the same story wherever they go. I thought the others' antagonism was because she was new. Perhaps I was wrong." He turned his attention back to Anna. "Disfigured in what way?"

She shrugged. "I'm not certain." Turning to her husband, she suggested, "Perhaps I should visit her?"

Barak was already shaking his head. "Not right now. Not in your condition." His eyes went to her rounded abdomen. "It won't be long now. I'd rather you stay close to the house."

Before she could answer, a small projectile flew across the room, landing on her thighs. At her small "oomph," Barak was already on his feet lifting a small boy from her lap. The child quailed at his angry voice.

"Ramoth! I told you to be careful around your mother!"

Tears pooled in the child's rounded brown eyes, an exact replica of those staring angrily into them. As usual, those tears were his father's undoing. Barak's voice gentled.

"You could hurt your mother, Ramoth. You wouldn't want to do that, would you?"

Dark curls tumbled about the little head as it shook vehemently from side to side. "No, Father."

Barak hugged his son and then set him on the floor. Father and son stared into each other's eyes a moment before Barak's lips tilted into a smile. The answering one on the boy's face was instantaneous.

Anna sighed as goodwill was restored between the two. Sometimes she thought her son was an accident just waiting to happen. Looking at him now, her mother's heart melted. No matter how much trouble the little five-year-old got into, she loved him with a passion.

"Are you ready for bed, my son?" she asked him.

For a moment his eyes turned a mutinous amber, but one look at his father and he dropped his head. "Yes, Mother."

Adonijah grinned as he watched the two depart. Ramoth's hand was tucked into his mother's, his head tilted upwards as he chatted with the speed of a moving chariot. Anna's head was bowed attentively, her rounded form waddling along at the boy's side. Her plain features were made almost beautiful by the love glowing on her face.

Suddenly, Adonijah's eyes grew misty and the smile slowly slid from his face.

"You're a lucky man, Barak."

One dark eyebrow lifted in inquiry. "Luck, Adonijah?"

Adonijah had the grace to blush. "My apologies. I should have said that you are truly blessed."

Barak nodded. "Indeed. Jehovah has been very good to us."

Without thinking, Adonijah answered him absently. "Us?"

Barak returned to his seat at the table, his serious gaze directed on his friend. "What is it, Adonijah? What's troubling you?"

Sighing, Adonijah shrugged. His lips twisted into a grimace. "I don't know."

How could he explain that every time he watched Barak and his family together, he felt a restless longing inside that seemed to have no solution?

As though he could read Adonijah's thoughts, Barak answered him. "Your turn will come, Adonijah. In Jehovah's good time, your turn will come."

Brown eyes met brown eyes, and a message was sent and received. Adonijah grinned ruefully.

"I'm almost thirty years old, Barak."

There was a twinkle in Barak's eyes. "Truly an old man."

Lips twitching, Adonijah rebuked his friend. "That's easy for you to say. You *have* your family and a place to call home."

"You are always welcome as part of our family." No trace of humor remained.

Adonijah got up from his seat. Placing a hand on Barak's shoulder, he stared somberly into his companion's eyes. "I have never doubted that, my friend."

They shared a silent moment of communication before Barak nodded his head. "I understand. If you wish, Anna and I will pray about it."

For a moment, Adonijah just stared at him. Why hadn't he considered that route himself? Briefly, he nodded his head.

As Adonijah was about to leave the triclinium, Barak asked him, "What made you notice this particular girl in the fields today?"

Adonijah's back stiffened, his hand resting on the doorway arch. He answered over his shoulder.

"I'm not certain. She was. . .different."

Walking away, Adonijah missed seeing his friend's slow smile.

⁂

Adonijah threw himself onto his bed, folding his arms behind his head. He stared upward at the ceiling and watched as a cricket moved across its white surface.

Mara. The word itself meant "bitter." Why would a mother give a child such a name? Had she known the kind of life her daughter would lead? Or was she perhaps expressing her own feelings for the birth of such a child?

What kind of disfigurement did the girl have, anyway? He had once seen a man whose face had been disfigured by fire. It had been a gruesome sight.

In his mind's eye, he could still see the hostile looks of the other gleaners as they moved around the woman. Pity welled up inside of him. Quickly he sat up, shoving his head into his hands.

Why should he feel such an overwhelming burden for this woman? He tried to push thoughts of her away, but they refused to be budged.

Reaching over, he blew out the lamp beside his bed, quietly staring into the darkness as the smoke drifted around him. The words of Solomon sprang to his mind. *Charm is deceptive, and beauty is fleeting; but a woman who fears the Lord is to be praised.*

Did this woman fear the Lord? Did she perchance know Jesus? If not, should he try to talk to her about Him? If anyone had a need of his Lord, it would be someone like this Mara.

Surely it wouldn't be unseemly for him to talk to the woman. Didn't he try to talk to *all* who came to glean in his fields?

Lying down again, he rolled to his side and watched the moon through the balcony doorway. His lips twitched as he remembered others he had spoken to about Jesus. Some were horrified; others were willing to listen. Then there were others who never set foot in his fields again. Some of those same people ever after avoided him as though he had leprosy.

The soft scent of the blossoming hillsides came gently to him with the cool breeze blowing in the doorway. Sighing, he closed his eyes and began his nightly petition.

Father in Heaven. Holy is Your name.

He could always try to speak to the woman when she came to the field tomorrow.

Your kingdom come! Your will be done!

Was it perhaps Jehovah's will that he talk to her? Why else should he feel such a responsibility? Irritated with himself, he tried to focus his mind on the prayer that the Apostle Philip had taught to them.

Give us this day our daily bread.

Did Mara have enough bread? Had she gleaned enough in the field today for herself and her grandmother? Gritting his teeth, he commanded himself. *Concentrate!*

Forgive us our debts, as we forgive our debtors.

People like Mara had so little, and often they became deeply in debt. He had heard of parents selling their children to pay for their obligations. Many women sold *themselves* to pay their debts.

Lead us not into temptation.

He certainly had no concern there. Jehovah had put a burden on his heart for this woman, and somehow he would have to find a way to help, but he knew he would have no problem with temptation. Remembering the man with the burned face, he shuddered.

Deliver us from the evil one.

Satan. The morning star. Roaming about the earth trying to destroy all that Jehovah had created. He was everywhere, yet no one could see him. Just like Jehovah. The only way to recognize either one was by their representations on this earth. Good comes from Jehovah, but evil comes from Satan.

Yours is the kingdom, the power and the glory. Forever.

Tomorrow he would seek out this Mara in the fields and find out if she knew his Jesus. If not, he would take great pleasure in telling her about Him. So far, he had done little to spread the Word. Now was his chance to right that wrong.

I hear You, Lord. I will be Your mouthpiece. Send me where You will!

In Jesus' name. Amen.

two

The morning sun shone brightly against the spring landscape, a precursor of another warm day. Adonijah watched with rapt attention as the reapers grabbed handfuls of grain and then expertly sliced them at the base with the sickles they wielded so effortlessly. The blades flashed in and out, the sunlight reflecting off their gleaming surfaces.

Helpers followed along in their wake, bundling the wheat into bunches and tying them with hemp cord. They then handed the sheaves to other workers who loaded them onto wagons to be moved to the threshing floor. The constant movement of people as they went about their jobs reminded Adonijah of ants as they scurried about their own business.

The whole operation was smoothly and skillfully administered, and Adonijah was again filled with an acute sense of pride.

When the harvesters had cleared an area, they would motion for the gleaners waiting anxiously on the sides of the field.

So many women and elderly, Adonijah thought, watching them bend among the fallen grain. Although gleaning allowed them to have food, it was an arduous job.

He searched among the gleaners, remembering his promise to the Lord from the night before. His troubled brown eyes scanned the area, trying to locate the woman from yesterday. Although there were many with frayed brown robes and veils, he knew that none of them was Mara. How he could be so certain, he didn't know, but there was no doubt in his mind.

A twinge of anxiety brought a quick frown to his face. He had absolutely no idea how to go about locating the woman.

He grew unreasonably irritated with her for not being where he thought she should be.

He was about to turn and head back to the villa when a thought struck him. Perhaps something had happened to her. Suddenly, he remembered the ill-concealed dislike of the other gleaners.

His eyes took on an icy sheen as he studied the other gleaners going about their task of providing for their daily meal. Face settling into lines of grim resolve, he headed for the nearest woman.

At his approach, the woman looked up. Anxious brown eyes regarded him warily before she quickly cast her eyes to the ground. She waited for him to speak, starting at his anger-filled voice.

"Do you know the one they call Mara?"

Eyes wide with fright, the woman hastily shook her head. Adonijah could see the trembling of her hands as they clutched her wheat-filled veil. Taking a deep breath, he tried to calm himself. His voice became milder in an attempt to soothe the woman's fear of him.

"They tell me that she is disfigured in the face?"

Sudden comprehension flooded the woman's features. She nodded briefly.

"I know the one to whom you refer. I did not know that her name is Mara." A malicious smile touched her lips briefly. "An appropriate name."

Adonijah's bland face concealed his disgust. He waited a moment to gain control of his feelings before he tried again. "You know where she is?"

"No, Master. I have not seen her today."

The woman studied him curiously, obviously wondering about his interest. Perhaps she hoped that he would expel Mara from the fields. Refusing to answer her unasked question, Adonijah turned and left her gaping at his retreating back.

Adonijah felt his frustrations mount. How could he find the woman? For that matter, why should he even want to? He felt a niggling sense of worry, but there was really nothing he could do right now. Perhaps she would come to the field tomorrow and he could search for her then.

Settling the matter in his mind, he pushed thoughts of her from his head and turned his steps toward the threshing floor. Although he trusted most of the workers, it was still his job to see that things were managed well. There was one thing every laborer who worked for Barak knew, and that was that he, Adonijah, would not tolerate any improprieties. His tolerance level for any kind of abuse was extremely low.

He retrieved his horse from where he had left it, and giving one last glance over the fields, he set his horse galloping towards the outskirts of town where the high, flat mound of the threshing floor was situated.

&

Mara watched the healer as he added some ground willow bark to a cup of water and quickly stirred it. His eyes flicked briefly towards her before he once again concentrated on her grandmother.

"You needn't cower in the corner, girl. And you needn't try to hide your face from me. I've seen much worse than you in my time."

For the first time, his narrowed gaze focused unwaveringly on her face, catching her unwilling eyes. "You should thank Jehovah that you are as well off as you are."

His words awoke an anger deep within. Although elderly, he stood before her strong and capable. He had all of his limbs, and there were no unsightly marks upon his body. She wanted to shout, *What would you know about it?* But she remained silent, her lips pressed tightly together. Pity and anger she had encountered often in her life, but never this arrogant acceptance.

The healer shook his head slightly as he began to gather his things together. Mara could tell he wanted to say more, but instead, lifting his eyes to stare directly into hers, he handed her a small pouch. His faded brown eyes were filled with compassion.

"There is more willow bark powder inside. Mix some with water and give it to your grandmother again when the sun reaches its zenith, then once again before she sleeps for the night. It should help to relieve her fever."

She took the pouch from him, dropping her eyes to the rough dirt floor. Feeling guilty at her earlier uncharitable thoughts of the man, she told him, "Thank you. I have no way to repay you."

The healer hadn't missed the lack of comforts in this small hut. It bothered him that the old woman had no blanket to keep her warm. Both women wore rags for clothing, and he knew that they would suffer come winter. He would have to find a way to do something. He had no doubt that Jehovah would arrange something. Why else had He sent these two women here? For the first time, the weathered old face creased into a smile. "Jehovah will repay me."

Mara didn't understand what he meant. Puzzled, she followed him to the door.

"I will return this evening to see if the fever has diminished," he told her.

Relief flooded through Mara. "Thank you."

The healer's eyes went once again to Mara's cheek, but she quickly gathered her veil close to her face. When his eyes met hers, she was surprised to find his filled with sympathy instead of revulsion. Turning, he left her.

❧

Adonijah watched the oxen as they tread the grain, the threshing board bumping along behind them. Briefly, the board flipped over and the iron spikes were exposed.

Instantly there was a shout, and the oxen stopped. Taking the opportunity afforded them, the beasts began to munch on the grain at their feet. Since Jehovah himself had commanded it so long ago to Moses, they were allowed to graze undisturbed.

The driver swiftly flipped the board to its original position and then climbed onto it, thereby adding his weight to keep the board stabilized. Snapping the reins, the oxen again began to move in unending circles around the wheat-filled threshing floor, the driver now standing with his feet braced apart on the bumping board.

As the board separated the golden kernels of wheat from the stalks, the winnowers would lift the threshed stalks with their winnowing forks. When the heavy grain fell to the ground, the chaff would be blown off in the wind. Over and over, the winnowing forks lifted and fell.

Adonijah felt the stiff breeze that blew against his perspiring brow. Brushing the damp, dark curls from his forehead, he smiled. It was definitely a good day to winnow.

Several women with sieves were sitting and standing among the piles of grain to separate the chaff even further. As they shook the sieves, the heavy grain would fall through the small holes while the chaff remained behind. They laughed and chatted while they worked.

One young woman attracted Adonijah's eye, her slow smile catching him by surprise. He knew that she was related to one of the male fieldhands who had been hired for the harvesting. Everyone from those families would be helping to harvest the fields, since all would reap the benefits.

Her dark eyes shone luminously with reflected sunlight, and although her skin was darkened by that same sun, it was still smooth and flawless. She was extremely attractive, but Adonijah felt only a passing interest.

Before, he would have tried to find out who she was, for

he was still young enough to enjoy a mild flirtation. But something about his thoughts and feelings had changed lately. His lack of admiration brought a small pout from the neglected lady when he turned and walked away.

Shrugging, Adonijah made his way over to where the grain was being poured into clay jars. He counted the marked ones being set aside for the tax collectors and realized that Barak would still have a considerable harvest left over.

Simon, the tax collector, was a wily man, but at least he was more honest than most. Although he charged a surplus for his own benefit, it wasn't anything compared to most of the tax collectors in the area. Simon had grown to be a wealthy man through dishonest gain, but then he had accepted Jesus as his Lord. Now, although Simon still charged over the tax amount, he used most of his profit to help those less fortunate. What made him such an unusual man, and a favorite among the Romans, was that his keen reading of a person's character kept everyone who had to deal with him honest, Roman and Jew alike.

Pounding hooves drew Adonijah's attention, and he watched in surprise as Emnon, one of the estate owner's bodyguards, came hurtling towards him. The man jerked back so hard on the reins, the startled horse reared.

Grabbing the reins, Adonijah tried to help Emnon soothe the beast. The Philistine's dark eyes glittered with anxiety and his face was strangely pale.

"It's Lady Anna. Her time has come. I have to go for Tirinus, but Barak asks that you go for the healer."

The color drained from Adonijah's face. Something must be seriously wrong for Barak to require the healer. Normally, only the midwives were called for a birthing. Before he could ask questions, Emnon whirled his black horse about and raced off across the green fields.

Adonijah watched him mere seconds before he mounted

his own horse and turned it towards the village. Digging in his heels, he sped off in the opposite direction from Emnon.

When he arrived at the healer's house, the sunlight was already beginning to weaken. He pounded on the door furiously. It opened almost at once; an old woman, her weathered face twisted with surprise, peered out at him.

"Martha, I need to speak with Likhi."

"He is not here. Is something wrong, Adonijah?"

Adonijah impatiently tapped his palm against his thigh. Martha's eyes followed the nervous movement, and he forced himself to be still.

"It is Anna's time. Something must be wrong, because Barak sent me for Likhi."

Her face contorted with pity. "I'm sorry. He went to the poor community to check on an old woman who is sick with fever."

"The poor community?" Narrowed eyes followed the direction of Martha's pointing finger. "I will go there, then."

She shrugged helplessly. "I don't know which house it is."

Adonijah was already remounting his horse. "I'll find it."

ஃ

Mara watched the healer's face intently, searching for any sign of misgivings. He turned a smiling face to hers, and Mara forgot about her own marked face. She returned his smile hesitantly.

"She is well?"

"Well. . .not quite," he protested. "But it would seem the fever is responding to the brew."

Mara was filled with such overwhelming relief that she impulsively hugged the old man. For a moment, she clung to him, tears of happiness crowding her throat. She swallowed convulsively, trying to find words of gratitude.

Likhi patted her shoulders awkwardly until she quickly moved from his grasp. Lifting the hem of her ragged tunic, Mara rubbed furiously at her eyes.

Twinkling brown eyes watched her face color hotly as she realized what she had done. Seeking to relieve her of her embarrassment, he grinned.

"Now, now. None of that. I'm a married man."

When she realized that he was jesting with her, Mara's lips twitched slightly. He was a kind old man, and she liked him more each time they met. There was something different about him. She wondered what it was that caused him to be such a loving, caring man. She had not met many, if any, such men in her time.

Her face remained a fiery red, causing the purple mark to stand out more clearly, and although she felt more comfortable in his presence than she did with most people, she swiftly maneuvered herself away from his careful scrutiny.

"Would you like a cup of water before you leave?"

He smiled gently. "I would like that very much."

Mara poured them both a cup, motioning for Likhi to be seated at the small table. Her grandmother's chair creaked alarmingly with the old man's weight, and Mara hoped it wouldn't choose this time to fall apart.

They both gazed at her grandmother's sleeping form.

"Tell me, Mara. Where are you from?"

Likhi watched the closed expression cover her face. He hadn't meant to be nosy, but he *was* curious. "You don't have to tell me if you don't want to," he remonstrated softly. "I just thought that you might like to talk."

It had been so long since she had talked to anyone besides her grandmother that Mara wasn't certain she would remember how.

"We're originally from Medeba."

He looked his surprise. "Near Jerusalem. Have you family there?"

Mara shook her head. "Not anymore."

In actuality, there were several relatives there, but none

that would claim Mara or her grandmother. Well, maybe Grandmother, but Mara knew her grandmother would never forsake her, not even if it would make life simpler for herself. Feeling a fierce desire to protect her grandmother, Mara glared at Likhi.

"We have only each other."

Likhi watched her closely for several seconds before he asked, "If you don't mind my asking, why have you come to Sychar?"

What could she tell him? That Sychar was the next stop along a path of dozens of stops? That any place was only temporary as far as they were concerned? That even though Samaria was anathema to most Jews, it couldn't be filled with any more hate than they had encountered elsewhere?

"I do mind," she told him, getting up and crossing to her grandmother's side.

Recognizing his error, Likhi changed the subject.

"You have been gleaning in the fields?"

Mara nodded, her eyes never leaving the elderly form lying on the mat. "In the fields of a man named Barak."

She didn't see the healer's sudden start at mention of the name. A slow smile spread across Likhi's face, although a crafty look entered his eyes.

"Barak is a fine man, as is his manager, Adonijah."

"I wouldn't know. I have never met them."

Mara's look met Likhi's again, and she was surprised to see him glance quickly away. For a time, she had believed him different from others, but in actuality he was not. Although he claimed to have seen faces much worse than hers, he still could not gaze at her for long.

The silence grew uncomfortably long as Likhi scrambled around in his mind for something else to say. He had just opened his mouth when they heard thudding horse hooves on the path out front.

Mara moved quickly towards the doorway, stopping abruptly as an immense figure loomed in the opened portal. Sucking in a shocked breath, she placed one hand over her pounding heart, taking a quick step backward.

Likhi had risen to his feet and now was a reassuring presence behind her. Mara heard his surprised voice over her shoulder.

"Adonijah!"

Mara looked a long way up into astonished brown eyes. Although Adonijah had been staring at Mara, he now quickly turned his attention to the healer. Mara took the opportunity to cover her disfigurement with her veil. She retreated to the far side of the hut, away from the sunlight.

"Anna needs you," Adonijah implored. "Can you come?"

Without waiting for explanations, Likhi had already reached to the table to retrieve his pack of medicines. He hurried to the door. Frowning, he snapped at Adonijah.

"Well, don't just stand there. Move!"

Adonijah had been watching Mara as she huddled in the dark. Startled by Likhi's words he moved to the side, allowing the healer to pass. His wits had been scattered ever since the first moment he had come face-to-face with the woman he had been searching for all day.

He glanced at her now, briefly, before following Likhi from the hut.

Mara watched them leave, her mind in a fog. Although Adonijah had seemed surprised, she had seen no censure in his eyes. What had stunned her most was that for the first time in her life, she had felt an instant attraction for a man. And a lot of good that would do her! Although he hadn't looked at her with loathing, neither had he shown her anything else. After that first surprised look, his face had gone carefully blank.

She hurried across the room and watched from the shadows as Adonijah mounted his horse, reaching down a hand for the healer. Lifting Likhi effortlessly to the seat behind him, Adonijah's broad shoulders rippled against his tunic. Even from a distance, she noticed the gleam of his eyes that hinted at hidden amusement.

My, but he is handsome! For a moment Mara allowed herself a fanciful daydream where she was completely normal and Adonijah had looked at her with instant attraction, too.

Although she giggled, there were tears in her eyes when she finally retreated from the window.

❧

Likhi reluctantly placed his hand in Adonijah's. Adonijah hid a grin as he pulled the healer up onto the back of the horse. Well could he remember his own aversion to the huge beasts. Being a farmer, he was used to oxen, but only for driving. Never had he ridden any creature before coming to Samaria. Now, riding a horse was as normal to him as walking.

"Hold on, Likhi."

It was obvious that Likhi had no intention of doing anything else. Having a full-grown man cling so tightly to his midsection caused a restriction of airflow to Adonijah's lungs.

"Not *that* tightly!"

Likhi loosened his grip only slightly, and Adonijah resigned himself to an uncomfortable journey.

As they raced towards the villa, Adonijah's mind was in a frenzy. If anything happened to Anna, he wasn't sure what he would do. Barak would be devastated! And what of little Ramoth? Glancing over his shoulder, he saw Likhi's eyes closed, his lips moving in prayer. Whether for safety on this ride, or for Anna, Adonijah had no idea, but he began a frantic petition of his own.

For a moment his thoughts were diverted by the image of surprised brown eyes. When he had come face-to-face with Mara, the first thing he had noticed had been the huge colored mark on her face, but then his look had been arrested by the pain in those lustrous brown eyes.

The disfigurement hadn't been anything like what he had expected, but it was hard to miss. Why would Jehovah allow such a thing to happen to an innocent young girl? Her life must have been tragic as a consequence.

Then he remembered a story the Apostle Philip had shared with them. A man had been blind from birth, and the disciples had asked Jesus who had sinned to cause it, the man or his parents. Jesus had answered them that neither had caused his blindness, but that it had happened to show Jehovah's glory. Jesus had then healed the man.

But why had Jehovah allowed such a thing to happen to Mara? Had her parents sinned, and Mara borne the price? He had never understood the problems inflicted on humanity, and he had long ago given up trying to fathom things out. Of one thing he was certain: Jehovah was in control and absolutely *nothing* happened without His consent. When one studied the scriptures, one could see the Lord's fingerprints on every moment of time.

Still, he felt sorry for the woman. Although she had quickly veiled her expression, he had not missed the intense pain in her look. It had caused an unusual effect in his midsection, and he had wanted to reach out and relieve the agony from that wounded heart.

Likhi's loud voice brought him quickly from his thoughts.

"What is wrong with Anna?"

Adonijah shook his head. He, too, had to yell above the thundering of the horse's hooves. "I don't know. Emnon reached me in the fields and sent me after you."

"When we get to the villa, you must contact the others and start a prayer session."

Nodding, Adonijah agreed. "I will do so."

"And, Adonijah," Likhi continued. "Add Mara's grandmother as well."

Glancing quickly back over his shoulder, Adonijah briefly met the healer's eyes. They shone with an incredible faith, and something else as well. Adonijah recognized that look from previous occasions. Likhi was plotting something!

Turning back to the road, Adonijah kept his thoughts to himself as they approached the villa.

When they reached the villa, Likhi swiftly dropped from the horse's back and hurried inside. Adonijah followed just as rapidly, his steps faltering at the stillness of the huge house. Had he not known better, he would have thought the place deserted.

Remembering what Likhi had said, Adonijah searched for one of Anna's servant girls to send her with a message to the other believers. Having accomplished that purpose, he tried to find someone who could give him some information about Anna.

It took him some time to locate anyone, but he finally found Apphia, Ramoth's nurse, cuddling the little boy in the peristyle.

At his entrance, two pairs of frightened brown eyes lifted appealingly to his face. Ramoth struggled from Apphia's hold and ran to Adonijah.

Adonijah lifted the boy into his arms, settling him against his chest. Ramoth's bottom lip quivered and Adonijah could see the boy was struggling not to cry.

"What's wrong with my mother?"

Glancing swiftly at Apphia, Adonijah could see she had no better idea of what was transpiring than he. Trying to soothe the boy's fears, Adonijah spoke cheerfully, though it cost him great effort. "It's time for your baby brother or sister to arrive."

Apphia's voice quavered slightly. "Is there any news?"

Adonijah shook his head, throwing her a warning look at the same time. "No. We must wait."

Adonijah longed for some information about Anna and the baby, but he realized that there was a greater need here. Ramoth needed to be diverted from his fears, no doubt induced by the eerie silence of the villa.

Wrapping his arms securely around the youngster, Adonijah walked slowly towards the fountain in the center of the garden. "You look very hot, Ramoth."

For a moment the boy didn't understand. Glancing quickly in the direction Adonijah was headed, his intentions became clear. Ramoth's sparkling eyes meshed with Adonijah's, and his grip on Adonijah's tunic tightened. He said nothing, waiting silently as Adonijah drew up in front of the small pool.

Adonijah noticed the boy's lips twitching, his eyes full of eager expectation. Quickly, he lifted Ramoth over the pool before drawing him as quickly back to his chest. At the boy's small squeal, even Apphia's lips lifted into a reluctant smile.

Adonijah said nothing, his eyes boring into Ramoth's. They had played this game before. It was a question of who would surrender first. Adonijah continued waiting for Ramoth to ask, while Ramoth hoped to receive his reward without submitting to begging. For the moment, the boy had forgotten the tense situation in the villa.

Pretending to drop the boy, Adonijah grinned as he squealed again. Holding Ramoth mere inches from the water, he lifted him back against his chest.

The boy's eyes were now filled with determination. His lip curled out into a stubborn pout. Still, Adonijah refused to relent. Ramoth had a stubborn pride that brought concern to both of his parents, and Adonijah as well.

It seemed an eternity before Ramoth finally said, "Do it, Uncle Adonijah!"

Still, Adonijah waited.

Ramoth wriggled against Adonijah's hold, but although his grip was gentle, it was unyielding. Finally, Ramoth ceased his struggles. In a voice laced with irritation, he said, "Please."

Instantly, Adonijah dropped the boy into the pool. As Ramoth came up splashing and giggling, Barak entered the garden, his face etched into graven lines. His eyes fastened on his son and a brief smile touched his lips. Abruptly, the smile left his face, and Barak's eyes locked with Adonijah's.

"The baby has arrived."

Something was terribly wrong; Adonijah could see it in the agonized look his friend fastened on Ramoth. He swallowed hard, forcing the words past the lump in his throat.

"Anna?"

Barak turned on him a blank look. "Anna is well. But the baby. . ."

While Adonijah and Apphia looked on in shock, Barak lifted his son into his arms and began to sob quietly.

three

For three days, Barak's little daughter clung tenaciously to life, a sure indication of a strong will. Although prayers were being said in her behalf, a pall hung over the household. Many were saying it would be as well if the child died.

Adonijah watched the sleeping infant and momentarily wondered if they might be right. Since the child was free of the restricting swaddling clothes that wrapped most babes from head to foot, he was able to study her.

Her tiny head was capped by a swath of dark brown hair that felt downy soft against his exploring finger. Eyes closed in sleep, her little rosebud mouth worked furiously. Her tiny little face was angelic in its repose, and Adonijah felt a tug on his heartstrings.

His exploring fingers traveled past soft little legs, ending abruptly when his hands should have encountered a tiny little foot, with tiny little toes. Although her right foot contained just that, her left leg stopped where a foot should have begun. It was this that had others suggesting that it might be better if the infant died after all.

Adonijah frowned. What kind of hope for a normal life could a person hope to have as a cripple? Why had Jehovah let this happen, especially to a child of Anna's? Anna who loved Him beyond all measure.

Swallowing hard, Adonijah recalled that evening three days ago when Barak had entered the peristyle. Barak's tears had stunned him, but he had soon been made aware of the reason. Although the child lived, it was struggling to survive. And then had come news of its disability.

Even now, there were those superstitiously speaking of curses. Some had even begun to lay the blame at the door of the one called Mara. She was cursed with the mark of Cain, they said, and since Barak had allowed her to glean in his fields, the curse had transferred to him. Adonijah ground his teeth furiously, rejecting such an idea.

An even more preposterous idea came from the Samaritans living in Sychar who said it was Jehovah's anger against Barak for leaving his faith and following the infidel religion of the Christians.

Adonijah couldn't understand any of it, but one thing he did know: Jehovah had His reasons. As unfathomable as they might be, he truly believed that to be so. Didn't the prophet Jeremiah in the scriptures teach that Jehovah knew each person even in the womb? Didn't King David in those same scriptures teach that each person was fearfully and wonderfully made, knit together in a mother's womb? It said nothing about perfection.

He lifted the sleeping infant from her cradle and held her gently within his large palms. She was a tiny mite, and her restricted breathing rattled softly against the stillness of the room.

Anna and Barak had taken his offer to keep watch over the child so that they might go somewhere alone together and pray. For three days they had been fasting and praying, and now it seemed as though Jehovah had heard their petitions. Even Adonijah could tell a distinct difference in the child's breathing from only three days ago.

Adonijah curled the babe against his chest with one arm, allowing him freedom to trace her soft features with his other finger. As yet, the babe had no name. Barak and Anna wanted to choose right, hoping that Jehovah would give them insight into His will. Never would they name a child "Mara." Never would *they* consider it a bitter happening that their child was deformed.

The babe began to stir, her little fists moving against her chest. Adonijah stroked his finger down the little girl's arm and caught his breath in surprise when one tiny fist closed over it.

His eyes darkened with tenderness as he gazed on the perfect facial features. She would one day be a beautiful woman, but she was still deformed. Had the child been Roman, she would have been left on the rocks outside the city to die. Praise Jehovah she was given to Anna instead.

Adonijah felt a sudden, fierce desire to protect this little one from all harm. His heart swelled with an exquisite pain, and he knew without a doubt that he was completely lost. As surely as this child held his finger so tightly, so also she held his heart.

"Adonijah?"

Adonijah turned at his name, his swimming eyes meshing with those of the babe's mother. There was a question in Anna's hazel eyes as she watched Adonijah with the babe. She looked deep into the brown depths of Adonijah's eyes and sighed, nodding with satisfaction.

Adonijah's gaze focused on Barak standing protectively by his wife's side. As he and Barak stared at each other, as always, a message of understanding flashed between them.

When Adonijah could finally find his voice, it came out husky with suppressed tears.

"Have you decided on a name?"

Barak nodded. "Her name is Samah."

"Samah," Adonijah repeated, a slow smile settling across his features. "Yes, she will surely bring us all joy."

Anna crossed the room to his side, and Adonijah carefully handed the sleeping infant into her mother's waiting arms. Anna lifted troubled eyes to Adonijah's face.

"We have a favor to ask of you."

"Name it."

Barak grinned at his friend's lack of hesitation. "It has to do with a certain young man who is about to drive the whole household to distraction."

Adonijah returned his grin, chuckling low. "Perhaps my nephew would like to visit the threshing floor today," he suggested.

Anna frowned. "I'm not certain that's a wise idea."

All three knew the boy's penchant for making mischief, even when he didn't realize he was doing it.

Barak came to stand beside his wife. "I think we can safely entrust our son to Adonijah's care, my love."

"I did not mean to imply. . ." Color flooded her cheeks as she threw Adonijah an apologetic look.

Adonijah came to her rescue. "I know you did not. I will keep a close eye on him." He stroked a finger softly across Samah's rounded cheek. "If you do not mind, we will stay for the feasting tonight."

"The whole night?" Anna looked unconvinced.

"My love," Barak assured her. "It will give us time alone with our daughter. Likhi says that barring unforeseen circumstances, it looks like her breathing will continue to improve." His gaze met hers, and held. His voice was hushed when he continued. "It is time to end our fast and give thanks to Jehovah."

Adonijah felt like an intruder as he witnessed the loving exchange between the two. For a long time he had considered himself in love with Miriam, a Jewish girl from their old hometown of Jotapata. Now, after time and distance, he could see that what he had felt for Miriam had been mere infatuation. He longed for a love such as Barak shared with Anna. Even Barak's mother and father had had such a love. Would there ever be such a thing in store for him?

His thoughts wandered to the lovely girl from the threshing floor, but his mind instantly rejected her. Instead, his vision was filled with lustrous brown eyes from a disfigured face.

He shook his head to relieve it of such thoughts. What was the matter with him, anyway? Why was the girl Mara so often in his thoughts? Perhaps Jehovah was again trying to tell him that Mara needed a Savior. He hadn't had time to speak to the girl three days ago, and he certainly hadn't had the time or opportunity since. He must make a greater effort to see her.

"Adonijah?"

Jerked from his thoughts, Adonijah gave his friends a questioning look. Barak studied him a moment before speaking for the both of them.

"We agree. Ramoth may go with you."

"I will go find him to tell him," Anna told the two, and they silently watched her leave the room.

Adonijah knew that Anna would be giving her son explicit instructions on his behavior while he was in Adonijah's care. He turned to Barak, a slight grin lifting the corners of his mouth. The smile slowly disappeared at the look on Barak's face.

Adonijah squirmed under Barak's silent perusal. When Adonijah had been brought to Barak's family as a boy, Barak's father had adopted him as a son, first by verbal agreement, then by actual public announcement. Since that time, Adonijah had the right to call Ephraim, Father, and Barak, Brother. Although Adonijah had no actual blood connection to the family, it was amazing that Barak and he could read each other so well.

"What are you thinking?" Adonijah asked, his voice more peevish than he intended.

"I am wondering what has happened to change you so much in such a short time."

"Change?"

One dark eyebrow lifted upwards as Barak continued to watch Adonijah.

"I have never seen you so restless. There is something. . .I don't know, something *different* about you." Barak's eyes narrowed. "If I didn't know you better, I'd think there was a woman involved."

Adonijah's eyebrows disappeared under his curly bangs. "Don't be ridiculous! When have I had the time?"

Barak remained unconvinced. "It's hard to explain, my friend, but I recognize the look. It's as though you've been touched by someone, and you are as yet unaware of it." Barak frowned. "I know I'm not making any sense."

Adonijah lifted his cloak from a stool. "No, you are not. I will return in the morning with Ramoth."

Adonijah left the room feeling as though every part of his inner feelings had been exposed.

⁊

Mara watched the threshing floor from the hidden confines of a cypress tree. Already darkness had descended and the evening's feasting had begun.

She slid to the ground, crossing her legs beneath her. Normally, she was careful to keep to herself and stay as far from people as possible to avoid any unpleasantness that her presence often inspired, but tonight was different.

For the past three days, she had carefully fed her grandmother the willow bark brew that Likhi had left for her, and for the first time in days, Grandmother's fever was gone and she was sleeping a natural sleep.

Mara knew that her grandmother wouldn't awaken before morning, so she had succumbed to temptation and made her way outside the poor community to the threshing floor. She had learned only that morning that Barak's grain would be threshed for three more days before the crop from the next person would begin to be threshed.

Now, she watched silently as the field workers became lively in their celebration. Her mouth began to water as huge platters of food were passed around the group, and her empty stomach rumbled loudly.

Since she had been required to stay at home to care for Grandmother, there hadn't been time to glean in the fields. The little flour that was left she had used sparingly for her grandmother's nourishment, and now there was none left for the morrow.

Her eyes were suddenly caught by a large man winding his way among the reclining and dancing workers, a small boy child resting on his shoulders. She had no trouble recognizing Adonijah, even from such a distance. His confident bearing had attracted her attention more than once as she had gleaned in the fields.

He flipped the boy to the ground, their laughter echoing up to the hill on which Mara sat. Her own lips curled into a wistful smile as she watched them play. It had never occurred to her that Adonijah might be married and have children. The thought disturbed her more than she cared to admit.

Before long, she lost sight of them among the others, and her attention turned to a group of women dancing to the sound of the lyre. Their graceful movements filled Mara with a deep envy that she hadn't realized she possessed. Oh, to be free to act like a normal woman!

A waxing gibbous moon gave light to the surrounding landscape, along with the various fires that lit the threshing floor.

"Shalom."

Mara came to her feet in an instant, her hand clutching her tunic where her heart was pounding in a thunderous rhythm. Eyes wide with fright, she turned at the sound of the voice. A small boy stood behind her, his curious gaze focused unwaveringly on Mara's form. The semidarkness acted as a shroud, but still Mara pulled her veil close against her face.

"Shalom," she answered, glancing behind him to see if

anyone else was in the vicinity. Her questioning eyes returned to the boy. "You are alone?"

His little head nodded up and down. "Who are you? Why are you sitting here in the dark?"

Panic seized Mara. Surely someone would come looking for the child sooner or later, and there was no telling what their reaction might be to her presence here.

"I–I was just leaving."

"Why?"

She frowned. How could she answer the child without sounding demented, or causing him to flee in fear? Before she could say anything, the child offered his hand.

"My name is Ramoth."

Hesitating, Mara glanced first behind her towards the threshing floor, and then behind the boy to the darkness beyond. Still, no one came for the child. She reached out her own hand and clasped his forearm. For a small boy, his returning pressure was sure and firm.

"My name is Mara."

Ramoth's eyes widened in horrified surprise, and he took a hasty step backward. His little mouth opened and closed, but no sound came forth.

Since Mara knew the child could not see her disfigurement in the darkness, she was surprised at his reaction. Understanding was quick to follow at Ramoth's low spoken words.

"You're the one who made my baby sister cursed."

A familiar deep wrenching pain squeezed Mara's chest. It was always the same, no matter how far she traveled. Wherever she went, nothing would ever change. She should have known better than to come here. Stifling a sob, she pushed past the boy and hurried away into the darkness.

She hadn't gone very far before she realized that she was being followed. Hastening her steps, she tried to out distance her pursuer. There were always brigands in these hills looking for wayward souls to steal from and murder, and if not two-legged animals, there were the four-legged variety. A sudden thought brought her up short. *Surely the child wouldn't—*

"Mara, wait for me!"

The panting, labored voice was definitely that of a child. Mara stood still until Ramoth caught up to her. "Foolish child! You could be killed out here in the dark. Go back to your parents!" she said angrily.

Ramoth drew back from her, startled. Then his half-shadowed face set into a mutinous expression, his lips pressed tightly together. "My parents are at home! I'm here with my uncle Adonijah."

Mara looked at the child in surprise. This, then, was the child she had seen Adonijah with earlier. An unaccountable sense of relief swept through her at the realization that the boy was not Adonijah's son.

"Why did you curse my sister?" he demanded. As he stood with his feet planted apart and his hands on his hips, angry defiance flashed from the child's eyes.

Her own anguish caused her to lash out at the boy. "I didn't curse your sister! Go back where you came from."

"They said you did."

Sighing, Mara tried to swallow her own tormented feelings. After all, he was but a child repeating what others had told him.

"How is your sister cursed?" she finally asked.

Tears swelled into Ramoth's eyes. "She. . .she doesn't have a foot."

Her own misery diminished in the face of the child's obvious distress. Sympathy for the unknown child welled up inside of her. Seating herself on a large rock, she motioned Ramoth to come closer. His defiant pose deflated immediately. Hesitantly, he came towards her, stopping at least three steps beyond.

Mara pushed her veil from her head, allowing it to drop around her shoulders. Although the light from the moon was dim, it was enough for Ramoth to see the mark on her face. He didn't recoil in horror as she expected; instead, the boy's eyes lit with curiosity, and he moved nearer.

"Some people say that I am cursed because of this mark," she told him.

He looked up at her questioningly.

"You may touch it," she told him. Why she allowed it, she wasn't certain. Never before had she allowed anyone other than her parents and Grandmother to touch her face. She had the oddest feeling that it would somehow comfort the child.

Ramoth moved even closer, uncertainty obvious from his expression. Without hesitation, his fingers moved across Mara's cheek. "It's soft!" he exclaimed.

Her lips twitched. "It's only skin. Whereas you have brown skin, mine is. . .is purple."

His wide eyes lifted to hers. She could see him struggling to understand, and she sympathized with his confusion. The anger she was feeling ebbed.

"Come, we must take you back."

Getting to her feet, she took the boy's hand and started back in the direction they had just traversed. They were halfway to their destination when they heard a slight sound behind them. Mara felt the hair rise on the back of her neck. She had the uncanny feeling they were being watched.

A rock tumbled down the hill to their right and Mara tensed. Ramoth's hand started to tremble so she pulled him closer.

"What is it?" His quavery voice reflected the terror that was turning her own limbs to water.

"I don't—" She was interrupted by a low growl, and as they watched, a pair of glowing eyes reached out to them through the darkness.

Mara sucked in a frightened gasp.

A hulking figure took shape as it moved into the moonlight, its feral eyes gleaming at them from the safety of the rocks above. Mara swallowed hard, her lips beginning to tremble.

"It's a lion!" Although Ramoth was frightened, there was an excited urgency in his voice.

Mara spoke quietly, trying to keep from startling the lioness. Her voice was little more than a whisper, but Ramoth heard each word distinctly. "I want you to go back to the threshing floor for help. Move slowly and quietly."

Ramoth looked at her as though she had lost her mind.

"Go, Ramoth," she commanded.

Slowly, Ramoth began to move backwards. At the movement, the lioness switched her attention from Mara to the child.

"No!"

The big cat's gleaming eyes swung back to Mara an instant before once again focusing on the retreating boy.

Mara reached to the ground, lifting a stick with one hand and a rock with the other. She moved into the path of the lioness's vision and again the she-cat focused on her. Her fear for the child far outweighed her own terror.

"You will not have him," she almost snarled. An answering growl reached her only seconds before the cat prepared to lunge. The cat's intention finally penetrated her hysteria-numbed brain. For a brief moment, she stood frozen with indecision. But only for a moment. Screaming, she threw the rock with all her might. It connected with the lioness's chest and she roared in pain.

Mara watched mesmerized as the great cat's lips curled back to expose huge fangs. If she had wanted to get the beast's attention, she had certainly succeeded. She knew without a doubt that this was the boy's only chance for escape.

"Run, Ramoth!" she shouted, lifting the flimsy stick as the lioness charged her.

❧

Adonijah was trying to locate his nephew, and he was not in a good frame of mind. Certainly, he would keep an eye on the child! Assuredly Anna could trust him to care for the boy! Ha! That was laughable.

Growing more irritated by the minute, he promised himself that he would throttle the child within an inch of his life. Already his search had taken him beyond the perimeters of the firelight of the threshing floor and into the darkness beyond. He had been positive that Ramoth wouldn't have come this far, but his certainty was wavering fast.

He had just resigned himself to the fact that he was going to have to ask for help from the field workers when he heard a piercing scream. The blood in his veins turned to ice, the color draining from his face as various pictures of his nephew flashed across his mind. *Dear Jehovah! Please, no!*

For an instant, he couldn't move. Only when he heard a second scream did his legs obey his will. Without thought for his own safety, he ran in the direction of the last echoing scream. The thought briefly entered his mind that he had no weapon other than the knife in the belt at his waist. There had been no time to go back for another, more adequate, weapon, but he couldn't concern himself with that now.

He plunged around a corner and collided with an object in his path. As he tumbled to the ground, he realized that he was entwined with a small body.

Surprised, Adonijah lifted his nephew from the ground. "Ramoth!" His eyes scanned the small body for injury. Finding none, Adonijah became furious. He shook the boy none too gently, his teeth gritting in his anger.

"What were you screaming about? Never, never do that again!" Even now his heart was thudding like a war drum.

Ramoth pointed back the way he had come, his voice coming in broken gasps.

"Mara! A lion!"

Shock congealed Adonijah's thought processes. For a moment, it seemed that time stood frozen. Only Ramoth's urgent tugging on his arm brought him to his senses.

"Hurry, Uncle Adonijah! Hurry!"

Adonijah hesitated, filled with uncertainty. He couldn't leave Ramoth here because there might be other lions in the vicinity. He also shouldn't take him back, because he didn't know what to expect. A picture of Mara lying on the ground in a pool of blood forced him to make a quick decision. Jerking Ramoth into his arms, he began to run back the way the boy had appeared.

He had gone but a short distance when he came upon a lioness crouched over a bundle on the ground. His stomach clenched at the ghastly sight. Shoving Ramoth into a rock cleft, he ordered him not to move.

Pulling his knife from his belt, Adonijah quickly moved towards the big cat, shouting and waving his arms as he went. The adrenaline was pumping so furiously through his veins, it was as though he were seeing the creature through a red haze.

The lioness jerked backwards, hunkering down over Mara's prostrate form, her teeth baring as she tried to protect her prey. Adonijah lunged at her, slicing the air in front of her with his knife. Blood was dripping from the big cat's teeth, and Adonijah once again felt his own blood solidify in his veins, as he thought about the life that blood represented.

Disregarding his own safety, he attacked the creature, his knife slicing into her chest. The lioness screamed in pain but still refused to relinquish her downed prey. Animal and man faced each other, both determined to have the unmoving figure. .

After several moments of parrying to and fro, the lioness abruptly lunged at Adonijah. He waited until the last moment before driving his knife clear up to the hilt into the animal's chest.

When the lioness fell to the ground, the momentum carried Adonijah along with her. There was a brief struggle, and then the massive body shuddered and finally lay still.

Breathing heavily, Adonijah shoved the animal away from him. Getting quickly to his feet, he hurried to Mara's inert form. He turned her over gently, sucking in his breath at the sight.

The lioness's fangs had ripped through the thin fabric of her tunic, leaving gaping holes in her arm. Blood was flowing swiftly from the wounds. Taking off his coat, Adonijah wrapped the garment as tightly as he could around Mara's arms. Although she had other scratches and bite marks, these were by far the most severe.

"Is she dead?" Ramoth's voice was so high that it squeaked.

Adonijah lifted Mara into his arms. "No. Come, Ramoth. We must hurry."

Adonijah didn't give the boy time to answer before he was already striding away. As he looked into the marked face, the eyes fluttered open. Where before those eyes had glowed a luminous brown, they were now dulled with pain and incomprehension. Adonijah felt a strange stirring deep within him. The feeling was similar to the one he had experienced the first time he had beheld his little niece.

"Be still, little one," he told Mara softly. "You are safe."

Something flashed quickly through her eyes before the lids drifted gently closed.

Adonijah found it difficult to keep his eyes and mind on the surrounding terrain.

four

The group standing around the room watched Likhi intently as he ministered to the woman on the bed.

Anna held her son close against her thighs, dry tears on her face an indication of a recent weep. Ramoth's face was buried against his mother's skirt, his shoulders still shaking with his silent sobs.

"It's all my fault."

Ramoth's muffled voice broke the stillness of the room. Anna and Barak exchanged glances.

"I will take him and put him to bed," Anna told her husband. He nodded before turning his attention back to the bed.

"Will she live, Likhi?"

Adonijah was thankful that Barak had asked the question, for words were still beyond his capabilities at this point in time.

Likhi shook his head, his face grave. "It's hard to say. She has lost a lot of blood and she has some serious wounds. She is doing as well as possible for the moment." He turned to Adonijah. "Someone will have to see to her grandmother. You know where?"

Adonijah was loathe to leave, but no one else in the house, save Likhi, knew where the girl was from. His eyes met the healer's. There was a question there, waiting to be answered.

"I will go," Adonijah agreed reluctantly.

Barak followed him from the room. "Would you like a servant to go with you? Then you could return here."

Adonijah's face instantly lit with relief, but a frown was quick to follow. "Do you know of anyone who will be willing to go?"

"I will ask," Barak told him doubtfully. He, too, knew that the whispers of curses had grown louder.

"I will be in the courtyard," Adonijah told him, turning to go.

Adonijah struggled against a strong desire to go back to the sick chamber. His thoughts were as chaotic as a whirlwind. The girl had saved Ramoth's life. Never would he be able to repay her. The child had been his responsibility, and he had failed to uphold the trust he had been endowed with.

Guilt flooded his entire being. If not for him, perhaps the woman Mara would not now be in the state she was in. She had protected the child, perhaps at cost to her own life.

He lifted his eyes to the night sky. *Dear Jehovah, please give me another chance*, he pleaded as he attached his horse to the small cart kept in the courtyard.

Barak reached him a moment later, Apphia following in his wake. The girl lifted frightened eyes to Adonijah. Although Apphia was a Christian, Adonijah could tell that all the talk of curses had shaken even her.

Without a word, Adonijah helped Apphia into the cart, climbing up beside her. When he looked at Barak, he felt as though his friend were trying to read inside his mind.

"Send word if there is anything that you need."

Adonijah nodded. "I will do so."

Turning the horse, Adonijah slapped the reins to spur the animal into a fast trot. His eyes flicked briefly to Apphia.

"There is nothing to fear," he tried to reassure her.

Although she refused to meet his look, she nodded her head slightly. The rest of the trip was spent in apprehensive silence.

When Adonijah at last pulled up in front of the darkened hut, Apphia gave it one panicked glance before allowing Adonijah to help her from the cart.

Adonijah opened the door cautiously. There was no lamp inside, and although the moon was three-quarters full, it didn't penetrate far into the cramped interior.

Apphia waited at the door with the small oil lamp that they had brought with them until Adonijah carefully made his way to the back of the hut. When he had been here before, he had barely noticed the contents. He stepped softly, almost stumbling on the sleeping figure at his feet.

Kneeling quickly, he told Apphia, "Over here. Bring the lamp."

His voice roused the slumbering woman. Alarmed, she sat up quickly, clutching her tunic to her chest.

"It's all right," Adonijah soothed. "We are here to help."

It took some time to explain their presence to the old woman, and even longer to convince her that she was not well enough to return to the villa in the cool evening air. Mara's grandmother, though elderly and frail, certainly had determination of iron.

Finally, she agreed to allow Adonijah to return to the villa and bring her news as soon as there was any to report. Adonijah left the hut with a great sense of relief knowing that the woman would be safe with Apphia. Unhitching the horse from the cart, he quickly mounted and hastened back the way he had just come.

&

Likhi lifted Mara's eyelid and allowed it to drop back into place. Although it was still too early to tell much, there had been no change in the woman's condition.

Barak had left the room to go and tend to his family, and although there were those in this household who claimed to be Christians, there were none willing to sit with Mara. Since he couldn't leave her alone, Likhi settled himself in for a long night's vigil.

The pungent odor of the balm he had used on her wounds filled the air around them. The dim lamplight sending flickering shadows around the room did little to help relieve the pallor of Mara's face. Already the woman looked as one dead.

He studied the unconscious woman at his leisure. If not for the purple mark on her face, she would have been a beautiful woman. He had already witnessed her loving devotion to her grandmother, so he knew that there was beauty inside. The words of his Lord came clearly to his mind. *"Greater love has no one than this, that one lay down his life for his friends."*

Had the woman forfeited her own life to save that of a young child she didn't even know? If laying down one's life for a friend showed great love, how much more did it show when one did so for a stranger?

Time seemed to drag by. Likhi's head was just beginning to nod when Adonijah returned. Surprised, Likhi lifted sleepy eyes in question.

Adonijah barely glanced his way before concentrating on the still figure in the bed. He moved quickly to her side, his eyes going slowly over her in perusal.

Noticing the slight lifting of her chest, he turned to Likhi in relief. "She is still alive." There was a wealth of satisfaction in the words.

Likhi gave an affirmative shake of the head. "Yes, but only just."

"You look tired, Likhi. I will stay with the girl if you wish to rest."

Adonijah's look was once again centered on the woman so that he missed the surprised look that Likhi gave him. He also missed the satisfied smile that edged the old man's mouth.

"As you say, I *am* tired. I think I can safely leave the girl in your hands."

At his words, the color drained from Adonijah's face. Hadn't he heard those same words just this morning? And look where that had gotten them.

Adonijah sat on the seat that Likhi vacated. Without thinking, he took Mara's small hand into his own. "What should I do?"

Likhi removed a jar of balm from his bag and lay it on the bed beside Adonijah's arm. "Every hour the wrappings must be changed and this balm added to stave off infection."

After explaining everything that needed to be done and any signs to be watched for, Likhi took his departure.

For a long time Adonijah sat watching the motionless figure on the bed. Only her faint breathing gave him hope that she was still alive. He gently pushed the dark hair away from her face, allowing his fingers to slide over her deformity. He was as surprised by the silky texture of her skin as Ramoth had been.

"You must live," he whispered. "There is so much I need to tell you."

There was no response, but then he hadn't really expected any. Remembering a story that Anna had told him, Adonijah began to softly tell the story of the birth of Christ and mankind's final redemption. Once, when Barak had lain close to death, Anna had done the same for him. Perhaps it helped, perhaps not, but Adonijah decided that he had nothing to lose.

The real burden that lay on his heart was the need to ask forgiveness. If only he had taken his obligations more seriously. He knew how much trouble Ramoth could get into. Why, oh why, hadn't he kept a closer eye on the child?

And then his thoughts turned to the fact that it could have been Ramoth lying beneath the cat's fangs. If that had been so, they would never have seen the child again because such a lioness could have easily carried the boy away.

Groaning, Adonijah buried his face against the sheets.

Some time later, Anna crept silently into the room. She came to stand beside the bed.

"How is she?"

"The same."

The grief in his voice nearly broke Anna's heart.

"It's not your fault, Adonijah."

"Yes, it is," he answered dully. "I should have paid closer

attention to Ramoth. It could have been he." At Anna's quick intake of breath, Adonijah rose to his feet, his features wreathed in apology. He pulled Anna close, feeling her body shaking against him. "I'm sorry, Anna. I shouldn't have said that."

For a moment she stayed where she was, then she pulled out of his grip.

"We can never repay this woman for what she has done. If I live to be a hundred, I will never cease to praise Jehovah for bringing her to this community."

Adonijah silently agreed. He watched Anna leave the room, then took his place on the stool. If Anna thought she owed the woman, how much more so did he? It had been a long and exhausting day, but sleep was the farthest thing from his mind.

❧

The morning sun filtered into the sick chamber, arousing Adonijah from the light doze he had fallen into. A quick examination showed him that there was still no change in Mara's condition. A servant brought a tray of food and quickly left.

Adonijah disregarded the tray. Although it had been hours since he had last eaten, the queasy turn of his stomach told him food would not settle well.

Anna came shortly after. "There is still no change?"

Adonijah shook his head. "None. Can you sit with her until I go to see her grandmother?"

"Barak will sit with her. I would like to go with you."

Though he was surprised, he didn't argue. "I'll get a wagon."

Anna met him at the wagon with a basket laden with food and several blankets. He smiled his appreciation.

"The grandmother is a proud old woman. I hope she will accept such gifts."

Anna's eyes sparkled with intent. "She will."

Adonijah hid a grin as he climbed up beside her. If anyone could reach Mara's grandmother, it would be Anna. She had a way with people, regardless of their stubbornness.

When they drew up in front of the hut, Adonijah chanced a quick glance at Anna's face. He didn't miss the look of pity that clouded her eyes. Without saying anything, she allowed him to help her from the cart and followed him to the door.

Apphia answered the door to their summons, her look of relief so obvious, Adonijah couldn't help but smile.

Anna crossed the room and knelt beside Mara's grandmother. Adonijah couldn't tell what was being said, but it was obvious that the old woman was impressed with Anna's gentle ways. She didn't hide the fact that she was a Christian from the old woman, but even that knowledge hadn't stopped the seemingly instant bond of friendship that appeared to have risen up between the two.

The old woman assented to staying at Anna's villa until Mara was well enough to return with her. Adonijah was amazed that she would do so, because it was evident that the woman was a devout Jew. Whatever her reasons, she had agreed to come, and Adonijah had the uncanny feeling that his life was about to change forever.

☙

Mara opened her eyes to intense pain. She moaned softly when she tried to move. Every nerve in her body seemed to be on fire.

Brown eyes dulled by suffering searched until they found the figure of her sleeping grandmother beside her bed. But this wasn't her bed. Her gaze ricocheting around the room, she realized that this wasn't even her home. Where was she, and how did she get here?

She tried to concentrate, to reason out the situation, but the only thing she could remember was ivory-colored fangs as they had sunk into her arm. And then had come excruciating torment like nothing she had ever known before.

Her eyes went back to her grandmother's sleeping figure. How had she come to be here? Grandmother had been so ill, and now she looked as though she were doing nothing more than having a good night's rest. There was even color in her wrinkled cheeks that Mara hadn't seen for some time due to their lack of nourishment.

Reaching out her hand, she gently stroked her grandmother's weathered cheek. The old eyes instantly opened, and her grandmother quickly sat up.

"Oh!" Her gnarled hands flitted about like a fly afraid to settle. "Praise Jehovah!"

Mara smiled faintly. "Grandmother, where are we?"

Tears streaming from her eyes, her grandmother gently clasped Mara's hand within her own.

"We are at the villa of a man named Tirinus. It's a long story, Mara. I will tell you later. Right now, I need to make everyone aware that you have finally awakened."

"Wait!"

Mara's grandmother turned at the doorway, her eyebrows raised in question.

"How long have I been asleep?"

"Too long," her grandmother answered fervently. "Now rest. I will return shortly."

Already drained of energy, Mara lay back against the pillows and stared at the ceiling. Strange images of a baby lying in a manger floated through her mind. Odd that she could remember such an unusual dream.

She glanced up in surprise as Adonijah came quickly through the door. The look on his face changed from one of uncertainty to one of satisfaction.

"You *are* awake."

Adonijah was followed by a woman. Her serene face was relieved of plainness by the beauty of her unusual hazel eyes. Confused, Mara stared from one to the other as she struggled to hide her birthmark.

"Shalom!" Anna greeted, disregarding Mara's obvious

embarrassment. "Our prayers have been answered."

"Prayers?" Wetting her dry lips with her tongue, Mara glanced from one to the other. "What am I doing here?"

Adonijah sat on the stool next to her. He wanted to reach out and touch her, but he didn't dare. With her wakefulness things had changed. He could already see the reticence returning to her eyes. She was trying desperately hard to keep her disfigurement from his sight.

"You were attacked by a lioness. Do you remember?"

Mara concentrated on the pictures growing clearer in her mind. One became vivid and sharp.

"The boy! Ramoth?"

Adonijah smiled widely. "He is well, thanks to you."

Anna came closer, and where Adonijah was reluctant, she was not. She picked up Mara's hand and squeezed it gently.

"We owe you our son's life."

Mara's embarrassment increased. "I did nothing," she told them, unwilling to admit that she had been watching the feasting at the threshing floor from her hiding place on the hill.

When her grandmother entered the room, Mara sighed with relief. She crossed to Mara's side and knelt by the bed.

"Child, I have been so worried."

Before Mara could respond, another man came into the room. He crossed to Anna's side and placed an arm around her waist, but his smile was for Mara.

"We can't even begin to tell you how happy we are that you are doing better, nor how thankful we are for all that you have done." Noticing Mara's drooping eyelids, he turned his smile on his wife. "But she must rest."

Anna wrinkled her nose at him. "I hear what you are saying. Come, Adonijah."

Mara felt a combination of relief and a keen sense of disappointment when Adonijah rose from his seat. Although no one seemed to mind her deformity, she was well aware that they had to be conscious of it. She was relieved that she wouldn't have to see Adonijah looking at her with pity, but she was disappointed that she wouldn't be able to watch him any longer. He was an extremely handsome man, and like any other woman, she was attracted in spite of herself. The only problem was, she *wasn't* like any other woman.

When the others had left the room, Mara turned her head slightly on the pillows so that she could better see her grandmother.

"They are kind people," she said.

Her grandmother glanced at the closed door. "They are that, but then they are Christians."

"Christians!"

Mara had heard tales of the Jews who had accepted a pagan religion. She remembered their being called Nazarenes, and although the group had been called "Christians" in a derogatory manner, they had chosen to keep the name that meant that they were "like Christ." It surprised her that her grandmother had spoken of them so fondly when she knew the truth. A cold shiver ran through Mara.

"We must leave!"

Her grandmother turned back to her, a small smile lifting her lips. She reached out a wrinkled hand and combed her fingers through Mara's tangled hair.

"No, child. In the first place, you are not well enough. And in the second place. . ."

"In the second place, what?" Mara prompted.

Sighing, her grandmother began to fidget with her robe. It was only then that Mara noticed that the garment was not her grandmother's.

"Where did you get the new robe?"

"Mara," her grandmother began hesitantly. "There is much I need to talk with you about, but now is not the time. I see the weariness in your eyes. You have a long way to go before you are well, so relax and enjoy Jehovah's blessing."

Jehovah? What had Jehovah ever done for her? From the beginning He had cursed her, and *now* He sought to bless her? Somehow, she doubted it.

"Grandmother—"

The old woman laid a restraining finger upon Mara's lips. "Hush now, child. Sleep, and we will talk later."

"But Christians, Grandmother!"

"When you are better, we will speak of this further. As you yourself said, they are kind people. Have any of the Jews you have known been as kind to us?"

Mara shook her head slightly.

"No," her grandmother agreed. "Wait to pass judgment until you are more fully prepared to deal with the truth."

The old woman got up to leave, but Mara clutched her hand.

"How long have we been here?"

"Five days."

Stunned, Mara watched her grandmother retreat from the room. Five days! Of all the questions churning around in her head, one stood out prominently: Had Adonijah seen her face exposed during those five days? Even the thought of it made her groan with disquiet.

The creaking door interrupted her thoughts. As it slowly moved inwards, a small, dark head warily appeared. Mara recognized the young boy at once.

"Hello, Ramoth."

He moved forward into the room, his steps suddenly sure and confident. He walked with the same proud bearing that Mara had noticed in his father.

"My mother said that I was not to bother you, but I wanted to say that I'm sorry."

"There is nothing to apologize for," Mara told him. "You did not cause my. . .my accident."

He dropped his head to his chest, his lips pushing out into

a pout. "I shouldn't have left the threshing floor. Uncle Adonijah told me not to, but I didn't listen."

Humor brought a sparkle to Mara's brown eyes. It was strange how she felt so comfortable with this small child. Perhaps it had to do with the fact that he treated her like she was a normal person. It was clear that her disfigurement didn't bother him in the least.

"Well, I shouldn't have been hiding in the hills, either. So maybe we have both learned a lesson."

Curious eyes lifted to hers. "Why *were* you hiding?"

Instantly, all humor fled. "I told you. People are afraid of me. They say that I am cursed."

Childish eyes glittered with anger. "That's not true! My mother said it is not true!"

"Your mother is a kind woman."

Ramoth nodded. "Yes, she is. She did not even beat me for the trouble I caused." He rubbed at his backside with his hands. "But my father did."

Mara grinned. "He did so because he loves you."

"That's what Uncle Adonijah says. He said if Father hadn't beaten me, he would have." The boy shrugged philosophically. "But I know they love me."

He came closer and gingerly sat upon the stool next to the bed. "I asked Jesus to make you well, and He did."

"Jesus?"

"You don't know Jesus?" His appalled voice brought another grin to Mara's face.

"No. Should I? Is he another healer like Likhi?"

Ramoth shook his head vigorously. "No, but in a way. He is Jehovah's son."

A cold lump settled in Mara's midsection. Now she remembered. The man that they called Jesus was believed by the Nazarenes to be the Christ, the Son of God. The child was speaking blasphemy! She opened her mouth to rebuke him, but was interrupted by a familiar voice from the doorway.

"Ramoth! What did your mother tell you?"

Adonijah glared at the boy before lifting his eyes to Mara's. Ramoth quickly vacated his seat and hurried to Adonijah's side.

"I only wanted to apologize, Uncle Adonijah."

For a moment, Adonijah said nothing. He was trying to read into Mara's expression, but her face had settled into an impassive mask. He could have sworn that the woman had recoiled in fear of him.

"I understand, but you still disobeyed. Go now."

Adonijah's eyes returned to Mara and found her trying to hide her disfigurement with the sheets. Their eyes met, and held.

"Don't," Adonijah adjured her softly. "You have no reason to hide from me."

Mara's hands stilled on the covers, her face filling with color. Searching Adonijah's face, she could see that he spoke the truth. He was not appalled by her disfigurement. She gave him a tentative smile.

Nodding his head, Adonijah turned to go.

"Good night," he told her quietly.

Mara watched him leave, the smile growing on her face. These were truly unusual people! She had never encountered such friendliness anywhere. Only the fact that they were Christians caused her any hesitation.

Sighing with lassitude, she closed her weary eyes. Sleep wasn't long in coming.

In her dreams, she saw a man, bloodied and flesh-torn, hanging on a Roman cross. His gentle eyes reached out to her in entreaty. Although His mouth never moved, Mara could hear His whispered voice in her mind.

"*Mara.*"

five

Adonijah stood just behind Anna, who was watching her father disappear down the road. She leaned against Barak, the tears evident in her eyes.

"He looks so old," she commented softly.

Recognizing her fear, Barak placed an arm around her waist. "The physicians said that he is well enough."

Tirinus had arrived as quickly as he could after receiving Emnon's message. Adonijah knew that the old man must have struggled with the decision of whether or not to return to Jerusalem. His granddaughter had quickly won the old man's heart, and only the realization that he was needed by his sister in Jerusalem had caused Tirinus to leave.

Although Anna had moved to this villa to be close to her father, he had in turn moved to Jerusalem after his sister had become ill. It was not possible for Anna and Barak to live there, knowing the Jews' hatred of Samaritans, and Anna's eyes gave away her heritage as surely as Barak's robe gave away his. For a Jew and a Samaritan to be married would horrify most Jews. Enmity between the two races had escalated to the point of insanity.

Adonijah had been willing to live in Sychar and farm their fields, but Barak had been unwilling to subject his wife to the growing danger in Jerusalem.

Adonijah turned to Barak after Tirinus was gone from their sight. "Will you go to Jerusalem for Shavuot as Tirinus suggested?"

Barak flicked a brief glance at his wife before turning his attention to Adonijah.

"I think not this year. Perhaps you would be willing to go in my place?"

Only two weeks ago, Adonijah would have been thrilled with the idea. Now he was filled with unexpected misgivings.

"Is that what you wish?"

"Someone has to make our thank offerings to the Lord. I can think of no other that I would trust more." His eyes met Adonijah's. "Do you not wish to go?"

An unexplainable sense of foreboding made him waver. Just for a moment an image of Mara's face came to his mind.

During the past week, he and she had developed a tenuous friendship. Sometime during that week, he had ceased to be aware of her deformity. Although it was an obvious affliction, it no longer bothered him. It hadn't taken him long to see past the abnormality to the woman within.

It was Likhi's last words to him that bothered him now. He had been on the point of leaving Mara's chamber for the last time, having pronounced her out of danger, when he had called Adonijah out of the room with him.

"Is something wrong?" he asked the healer uneasily.

"Not with Mara. It's her grandmother who concerns me."

"Bilhah?"

Likhi nodded. "I fear that her heart is not strong. The signs are there, though she tries to hide it."

Dismayed, Adonijah didn't know what to say. "Have you told Mara?"

Likhi shook his head. "No. I needed her to concentrate on getting well. Besides, if Bilhah wanted her to know, she would have told her."

"Why are you telling me?" Adonijah asked uncertainly.

"I don't know. I just thought someone should be made aware."

Now those thoughts, and the misgivings they inspired, returned to him in full force. His feelings of guilt, mixed with his genuine concern for the girl, left him feeling rather muddled. Although some were beginning to relax their fear around Mara, others were not, and they were inclined to say so. He really hated to see the girl hurt. She had won a place in his heart by her attitude with his niece, Samah. If it could be said, Mara was more fiercely protective of the child than Anna herself. Or so it seemed to him. Probably her own affliction had something to do with her affinity for the babe.

"If you would like me to go, I will certainly do so," Adonijah told Barak now.

"Good," Barak answered, and Adonijah knew the discussion had come to an end when Barak took Anna by the hand and returned to the villa.

Adonijah frowned at the colonnaded porch, allowing his gaze to wander over the large house. For six years, this villa had been home to them, but of late he had felt a yearning to have a place of his own. A family of his own. Although he didn't feel desperate about it, the longing was there, nonetheless.

His eyes opened wide in surprise when Mara came limping through the door, her grandmother holding her up. In two strides he reached Mara's side.

"What do you think you are doing? What are you doing out of bed?"

Mara opened her mouth to answer, but Bilhah interrupted her.

"She is as stubborn as a donkey, this one. She always has been."

Adonijah's dark gaze was delving deeply into Mara's brown eyes.

"We must go home," she told him, nibbling the edge of her bottom lip with her teeth.

The unexpectedness of the incident left Adonijah momentarily without words. He looked to Bilhah, and back to Mara.

"You are not yet well enough," he told her, irritation lacing his voice. "Where is your mind, woman?"

Mara's cheeks colored brightly, not from embarrassment, but from anger. The shine in her eyes would have warned her grandmother, but Adonijah had no idea of the hazard.

"If we do not go back to our home someone will think that the hut is abandoned, and they will move in."

Adonijah knew that she was right. That was the purpose of the community, to allow housing to the poor. Since the settlement was owned by the government, anyone was free to use it. If a hut was abandoned by one family, someone else was free to live there.

"There is still time," he began, but she interrupted him with a vehement shake of the head.

"No. We'll go now. I am strong enough. We will make do."

Short of throwing the woman over his shoulder, dragging her back to her room, and tying her up, there was really nothing Adonijah could do. His angry thoughts must have been reflected on his face, for Mara took a hasty step backwards.

Sighing, he brushed a hand through his curly hair, his eyes fixed on the road that led to their hut.

"I will get the cart."

"That's not necessary," Mara began, but was hushed into instant silence by the look on Adonijah's face.

Bilhah turned away to hide a smile. For the first time in her life, her granddaughter had met her match in stubbornness.

Adonijah left them standing there while he went in search of the cart. Mara followed his progress with smoldering eyes before her gaze returned to her grandmother's suspiciously quivering lips. Frowning, she refrained from comment.

Although Mara ached with every movement she made, the pain had diminished much over the past week. There were still a few cuts and gashes, but except for the one major wound in her forearm, they were healing well.

By the time Adonijah returned with the cart, Anna and

Barak had joined them.

"I wish you would consider staying longer," Anna told them earnestly.

Mara smiled briefly at her new friend, helping her grandmother as she climbed laboriously into the cart. Turning back to Anna, Mara reached for little Samah, her eyebrows lifted in question. Anna trustingly relinquished her daughter.

"You have been very good to us," Mara told them, her eyes focused on the babe, "but it is time for us to go home. We are very grateful for all you have done. We can never repay you."

"It's I who can never repay you," Anna answered fervently.

Barak handed Bilhah a covered basket. "Will you please accept this small token of our gratitude?"

Nodding, Bilhah reached down from her seat. She smiled her appreciation at all of them.

"May I come to worship with you this Lord's day?"

Although Adonijah and Mara were surprised, Anna and Barak were not.

"I will come for you," Barak told her.

Adonijah lifted a questioning brow at Barak, but Barak said nothing else. There was something happening here that Adonijah had been left in the dark about. He would have asked more, but Mara's face warned him to bide his time.

After Mara returned Samah to her mother, Adonijah helped Mara into the cart. Her lips were set in a tight line, her back as stiff as a shepherd's rod. Bilhah glanced at her once, but then retreated into silence at her granddaughter's fixed look.

Mara lifted her hand briefly in farewell before turning her face forward. There was a forbidding set to her shoulders, but since Adonijah was not a fainthearted man, he quickly opened the conversation.

"Bilhah, you have become a Christian?"

With a look, Mara dared her grandmother to agree. Bilhah ignored her.

"Barak baptized me in the spring behind the villa."

The smile that lit Adonijah's face transformed it from its earlier frown. "Praise Jehovah."

Mara's eyes kindled with fear. It occurred to her that her grandmother might have lost all reason. Not wanting to accept such a thought, she frowned from one to the other before turning her attention away from them.

Adonijah addressed himself to her. "And you, Mara? What do you think of Jesus?"

Although Adonijah had talked to Mara often about the Messiah, she had never given any indication that she had believed him. He had quoted the same prophecies that Barak and he had studied, but there had been no spark of interest apparent, save the one time he had thought there had been a strange yearning in her dark eyes. Mara had caught him looking at her, and she had quickly turned away. He hadn't seen that look since.

"An interesting story," she told him flatly.

Adonijah's brows drew together. "More than a story. Barak and I went on a pilgrimage ourselves, and came back believing. When you know the whole story, it's hard not to."

"Tell her," Bilhah encouraged, so Adonijah started at the beginning and told her their tale of salvation. He was still talking when they drew up outside the hut.

Although she pretended otherwise, Mara sat listening intently. Unconsciously, she lifted her hand to the left side of her face, stroking over the disfiguring mark. Suddenly, her eyes grew hard. She hopped down from the cart without waiting for Adonijah's assistance. Without looking at either of them, she hurried inside.

Bilhah sighed. "It will be hard to reach that one. She believes no one can love her, not even Jehovah." Turning his head slightly, Adonijah met Bilhah's eyes. Her wrinkled cheeks stretched into a smile. "Don't give up on her yet, Adonijah."

The look he fixed on Mara's retreating figure brought an instant sparkle to the old woman's eyes.

"She is a stubborn woman," Adonijah told her irately. "But I am not one to turn from a challenge."

Adonijah noticed the mysterious smile on the old woman's face as he helped her from the cart. She slowly waddled down the path after her granddaughter's retreating form, her voice floating back over her shoulder.

"I thought that you were not."

❧

Adonijah dropped down beside Bilhah, his eyes on the tall man standing in the center of the room talking to Barak.

"Mara refused to come?" he asked absently, watching as Barak and the man seated themselves next to Anna.

For the past three weeks Adonijah had spent a considerable amount of time teaching Bilhah and Mara about the man called Jesus, the Messiah. Bilhah opened up to the words of the great prophet, like a flower opening to the sun, spoken to them through the Apostle Philip. Mara, on the other hand, retreated farther into silence.

Although Adonijah and Mara had become friends of a sort, he could tell that she still shied away from too much close contact with him. It bothered him that her disfigurement caused her to retreat so much from life. After all, there was more to life than perfect features.

Before Bilhah had a chance to answer, Barak stood to his feet and addressed the Lord's day crowd.

"Brothers and sisters, welcome to our home. Anna and I are pleased to be able to share our home with other believers of The Way."

Barak smiled down at his wife before turning to address the crowd again. "You know that this is the day that the Lord set aside as a time to remember Him. As we partake of this supper that Jesus set aside as a memorial for all time to come, let us reflect on our Lord's death, burial, and resurrection. Jonathan will lead us in this most solemn occasion."

Barak resumed his seat beside Anna, and another young man rose to his feet. Lifting a tray with a loaf of bread, Jonathan asked them to bow for prayer.

The words, though softly spoken, brought a strange stillness to the room as each person concentrated on them. After ending his prayer, Jonathan passed the bread on the tray around the room and each person took a portion.

Bilhah questioned Adonijah with her eyes. He had forgotten to explain the ceremony of communion. Leaning close, he told her, "I will explain later. If you feel uncomfortable, you may wait."

She shook her head negatively. When the tray reached her, she took a piece of the bread and followed the example of the others as they closed their eyes in a reverent manner.

When Jonathan lifted the cup of wine, and declared it to be the blood of Jesus, Bilhah looked at Adonijah in horror. Jews were expressly forbidden to drink, or eat, blood. Adonijah could read the revulsion on her face. He leaned close again.

"It is only a symbol." He could tell she was still unconvinced. "Like the bitter herbs we partake of for Passover," he told her. "They represent the bitterness of slavery."

Slightly mollified, Bilhah wrinkled her nose slightly as she took a sip from the cup of wine. She quickly passed the cup to Adonijah.

When all had been served, Barak again rose to his feet. "Brethren, now that we have given honor to our risen Savior, let us continue with our evening meal."

He motioned for the servants to begin serving the prepared food. "At the same time, you know that we normally discuss the written scriptures of the prophets. But today, we have a visitor from Jerusalem who has brought us important words from the Apostle Paul and the Jerusalem council."

The quietness of the room was suddenly disturbed by voices raised in excited chatter. The tall man that Adonijah had noticed earlier rose to his feet to stand beside Barak.

"Brethren," Barak told them, "this is Silas, who has been sent by the Apostle Peter and the Apostle Paul with a message for the Gentile believers."

All sound ceased as each pair of eyes focused on Silas. Adonijah wondered what the council had had to say. Word had come to them that there was a dispute among the Jewish brethren and the Gentile brethren over the necessity of circumcision in order to be saved. Even here in this small congregation, where most were Gentile believers, the discussions had become loud and, sometimes, frenzied.

"Brethren of Sychar," he began. "I have in my possession a letter from the elders and apostles in Jerusalem. It is meant for those in Antioch, Syria, and Cilicia, but we are trying to share it with as many congregations as we can along the way."

The excited murmurs grew to a loud crescendo. It took some time before quiet was restored and Silas was able to continue.

"First," he told them, "I have some disturbing news to share with you. I would like to solicit your prayers on behalf of all Jews, Christian or not, who are from Rome. Emperor Claudius has expelled all Jews from the city."

Shocked and outraged, the crowd came alive in angry protest. Stunned, Adonijah's eyes met those of Barak across the room. Barak shrugged his shoulders, but Adonijah could tell that he was wondering the same thing as Adonijah himself. What could this portend for the rest of Palestine? Everyone knew that Romans loathed the Jewish people. Hatred had been brewing between them for some time now.

Silas continued. "Many of the brethren will be coming this way. I know you will welcome them when they arrive."

Adonijah considered his words. While it was true that many

of the *Gentile* Christian brethren would not hesitate to settle in Samaria, he doubted that other Jews would. Probably they would return to the holy city of Jerusalem instead, where they would be caught up in the persecution by the Jews living there.

After his speech, Silas then read them the letter from the Jerusalem council. When he came to the part about refraining from blood, Bilhah glanced at Adonijah with an "I told you so" expression.

When the time came to leave, the room was abuzz with discussions concerning the letter and the news from Rome. Since Barak was surrounded by so many people, Adonijah decided to take Bilhah home and explain the idea of the Lord's Supper to her. At the same time, he was hoping to get another chance to explain more about Christianity to Mara. He wasn't quite certain why it was so important to him that Mara believe, but it filled many of his waking thoughts, and sleeping ones as well.

The cart plodded along at a slow pace, the unprodded horse content to amble. For a while, Adonijah was quiet as he tried to gather his thoughts together. It was Bilhah who opened the conversation.

"I have noticed that here Jews and Gentiles worship Jesus together in harmony. What was the need of this letter from Jerusalem?"

Giving the horse a slap with the reins to spur him along, Adonijah smiled. "In Jerusalem, Christian Jews refuse to have anything to do with Christian Gentiles. Here, where so many are Gentile and the Jewish laws are not so strictly adhered to, we do not have that problem. Besides, there are very few Jews living here. Samaria is still anathema to most of them."

"And circumcision? Do you, too, believe that it is not necessary?"

Adonijah paused before answering, his brows drawing together into a frown. "As the Apostle Peter said, it has been a hard yoke for the Jews to bear. Maybe Jehovah intended it that way to make sure that His people were devoted to Him. I don't know. But too many scriptures teach of salvation for the Gentiles, and none of them speak of following Jewish edicts."

"What, then, makes the difference?"

"Jesus is worshiped in our hearts and minds."

Bilhah dropped into silence, and Adonijah returned to his earlier thoughts. The Apostle Philip had told them that Jesus himself had spoken of the destruction of Jerusalem. Would that then be the end of the Jewish nation? Was it possible that that beautiful holy city would one day be nothing but rubble? His Jewish blood rose up in protest at such a thought. The Jews had once been one of the mightiest nations on earth, but look where they were now. Still, now that the Messiah had been born, there was no longer a necessity to keep the Jewish bloodlines pure.

When they pulled up in front of the hut, Adonijah saw Mara circle to the back of the house.

"Mara must be fixing the evening meal," Bilhah told him, her eyes following her granddaughter's disappearing form.

"Didn't you tell her that you would eat with us?"

Bilhah threw Adonijah a look filled with annoyance. "The child has to eat, too."

Adonijah's lips drew into a tight line. "She could have eaten with us."

When Bilhah turned her birdlike eyes on him, Adonijah fidgeted under her look.

"Why don't you come in? I still have many questions, if you have the time."

Adonijah glanced toward the setting sun. "I can spare some time. It won't be dark for a while."

Instead of following Bilhah into the hut, though, Adonijah

turned his steps to the back of the house where Mara would be cooking her bread. He paused a moment to watch her as she bent over the small fire. She moved with such fluid grace that Adonijah wondered, not for the first time, what the woman would have been like without her marked face.

She had such a hard time believing that anyone could see past the mark. True, it was very noticeable, but Adonijah had become used to it and no longer felt uncomfortable about it. He treated Mara as he would any other woman.

"Shalom," he greeted.

Jerking around, Mara drew her veil close to her face. Relaxing slightly when she recognized her visitor, she turned back to her cooking.

"Shalom."

Adonijah moved closer until he was standing beside her. He felt again that strange sensation in his midsection when he was near her. Uncertain of its cause, he retreated to a safer distance.

"Why didn't you come with Bilhah today?"

"*I* am not a Christian," she answered, lifting her round loaf of bread from the fire pit.

"You would have been welcome anyway," he told her, annoyance in his voice.

Silence ensued for the better part of a minute.

"You had something you wished to discuss with me?" Mara finally asked.

Adonijah's voice deepened. "You know what I want to talk about."

Anger sparked in her deep brown eyes. When she was angry, she forgot to try to hide her face, and this pleased Adonijah. He studied her now, her ire bringing soft color to her face.

"Must you continue to harass me with all of this talk about a risen Savior?"

Taken aback, Adonijah frowned. Harass? Had he truly been harassing her? No, that was not so. He had only shared the good news with Bilhah and her, nothing more. In fact, it was Bilhah who often plagued him with questions of her own. Not that he minded. He was more than content to speak of the wondrous gift of Jehovah to mankind, although he still had much to learn himself.

His own anger rising, Adonijah advanced to her side. When she tried to hide behind her veil, Adonijah lost all reason. He jerked the veil from her fingers, throwing it to the ground.

Mara's eyes widened in amazement. For what seemed an eternity, she and Adonijah stared at each other. She recoiled from the blazing brown eyes glaring at her.

"Thunder! Leave that foolish veil alone!" Reaching out, he grasped her by the shoulders, shaking her slightly. "When will you realize that not everyone in the world finds you abhorrent? When will you realize that Jehovah has a purpose for your life, but He can't use you if you constantly hide yourself away? There is nothing wrong with you!" He shook her again for emphasis.

This only served to incense Mara further. She tried to wriggle free from his hold, but he was unrelenting. Pushing against his chest with her fists, she glared into his angry countenance.

"How dare you? What right have you to criticize me? You, standing there so strong and handsome! What would you know about it?"

At her words, some of the anger left Adonijah. Did she truly see him in that way? Handsome? In reality, he had never given it much thought. That she imagined him to be so brought a fleeting sense of satisfaction. He gentled his hold, pulling her closer so that he could better read what was in her eyes.

"Mara, don't you know that you are a beautiful woman?"

She snorted, interrupting what he was about to say. "Lying is a sin!"

She continued to squirm against his hold. He again shook her gently.

"Listen to me. You *are* beautiful. Your beauty comes from within, and it's a gift from Jehovah."

She dropped her head, covering her ears with her hands. "No!"

"Yes," he argued. "You don't want to believe it, but it's true. I think you like feeling sorry for yourself. It's easier to hide away than have to accept rejection. But if you don't take a chance, you will never know friendship. You will never know. . .love."

She glared at him, tears running in an unending stream down her cheeks. "No one can love me!" She brushed angrily at the tears on her face. For a moment, her whole being was filled with defiance. Suddenly, she sagged against his hold, a sob tearing at her throat. Her voice was little more than a whisper. "No one can love me."

Adonijah pulled her close, cradling her head against his chest. He wrapped his arms around her and held her until her sobbing quieted. The anguish in her voice was causing his stomach to twist into tight knots, and he wasn't certain how to help her.

"Shhh, Mara. You know that's not true." He tipped her face upwards, gently wiping the tears from her cheeks. He smiled, and she forced a smile in return.

"Your grandmother loves you. Anna loves you. Barak loves you. Jehovah loves you."

He paused a fraction before he added, "And I love you."

six

Mara turned restlessly on her mat. Although the temperature was pleasant enough, her thoughts were chaotic and wouldn't allow her to rest. A small pebble dug into her back, causing her to shift position yet again.

"Child, be still. Morning comes early."

"I'm sorry, Grandmother," she answered apologetically. "I can't seem to sleep."

Bilhah rolled over to face Mara, even though she couldn't see her in the darkness. There was a tenseness about Mara that transmitted itself to the old woman.

"What is troubling you, Mara?"

Mara turned her face away, afraid that even in the blackness her grandmother would see her telltale blush. The chirping of the crickets was the only sound discernable in the late hour quiet as Mara considered confiding in her grandparent. What would Bilhah say if she told her that her granddaughter thought she was in love with the manager of a wealthy estate? She smiled wryly to herself. Impossible.

"It is nothing."

Hearing the firmness of her granddaughter's voice, Bilhah knew that Mara didn't wish to discuss whatever was bothering her. Respecting her need for privacy, she reached out and patted her hand.

"Whatever it is, take it to Jehovah. His shoulders are much larger than yours, and can bear a far greater weight."

Mara frowned, listening as her grandmother turned back towards the wall. Jehovah? He was the mainstay of her problem. Could it be true that He really did love her? Why then would He curse her with such a face? And could it be true that He really did send His son to die for the sins of the world? The sacrificial lamb, once and for eternity, for all mankind? For years she had been taught that Gentiles were less than dogs, and now she was being told that the mighty Jehovah of the universe was offering salvation even to them. Not only that, but He had planned it to be so from the beginning of time.

Jehovah loves you. I love you.

Adonijah's refrain sounded through her head like a set of cymbals. She knew that he only meant that he loved her as a friend. Still, how long had it been since anyone, save her grandmother, had shown her such respect and kindness?

Then he had finished by saying, "And Jesus loves you, too."

Jesus. Greek for Joshua. In Hebrew they would have called him Yeshua. But this Jesus had been nothing like the Joshua of old, except for the mighty warrior's famous words to the people of Israel.

As for me and my house, we will serve the Lord.

This Jesus that Adonijah told them about had roamed the countryside speaking to Jews everywhere, telling them about the love of a being that heretofore had been only a frightening God who would one day wreak vengeance on the world. Jesus was sent to call Jehovah's people to repentance, and although Jesus spoke of a compassionate, loving Father, He was quick to point out that He was *Yahweh*. Holy of holies.

Even now Adonijah's earlier words burned in her mind. She had defiantly asked him what Jehovah had ever done for her. His responding anger had been frightening.

"What have *you* ever done for *Him*? You think that Jehovah is here to serve *you*? You think that you have only to command Him, and He should obey? Who was created to serve whom?"

Those fierce brown eyes had glittered down at her passionately and for the first time in her life, Mara had seen herself for what she truly was. Selfish, and ungodly. Her spirit writhed within her. It hadn't occurred to her before how blasphemous her thinking had been; it had taken Adonijah to point that out to her. At the time, it had made her angry, but now, she appreciated his willingness to correct her.

He had taken her gently by the shoulders, and through eyes swimming with tears, she could read in his face his genuine concern for her.

"I would not tell you these things if I were not your friend," he told her.

Adonijah was right. By shutting herself off from mankind due to other people's unkindness, she had allowed herself to become what her name implied. Bitter. Because of her own selfishness, her grandmother had had to suffer as well.

Yes, there were those who had treated her badly, and had condemned her family for misfortunes that were not their fault, but that was no reason to condemn the whole human race. That was no reason to slink off like a serpent and hide from the world. Surely she had more pride than that!

It had taken people like Anna, Barak, and Adonijah to show her the truth—people who truly worshiped the Lord, worshiped Him heart and soul. They served Jehovah by serving others, not themselves. Never had she encountered such unselfish people. They shamed her without knowing it.

She wanted to be like that. This Jesus, the one Adonijah called the Messiah, had suffered humiliation unlike anything she had suffered, and yet He had still remained faithful to Jehovah. He had unselfishly laid down His life for all of mankind. And Jehovah had given Him strength when He needed it most. Would He do the same for her?

She wanted so much to believe, but years of training held her back. Still, her grandmother was much older and wiser than she, yet Grandmother had accepted with faith the redemption offered her. The sound of even breathing came to her softly through the darkness, telling Mara that Bilhah was fast asleep.

There had been a difference in Grandmother lately. The worry lines that had etched her face so early in life were minimized now. There was a peace and serenity about her that Mara didn't understand. Their difficulties hadn't changed much over the last few weeks, but Grandmother faced them with a calmer outlook.

Mara quietly crawled from her mat and went to look out the window. A cool breeze blew gently across her face as she studied the moon. In a few days' time, it would be full again. A lover's moon.

Her thoughts inevitably turned to Adonijah. His arms had felt so safe and warm. She had wanted nothing more than to stay within their sheltered confines forever. She had known him such a short time, but it hadn't taken her heart long to recognize that he was the man she was destined to love.

For days she had been arguing with herself about her feelings. Never before had any man looked at her with any kind of affection. Even her father had spent more time away from home than with her. Now, a handsome man treated her kindly, and she thought she was in love. Was it possible that she felt mere gratitude? Or would she think herself in love with any man who treated her with polite thoughtfulness? How would she ever truly know? For that matter, what good would it do her if she did know for certain?

Sighing, she turned and went back to her mat. Trying to be as still as possible so as not to disturb her grandmother's peaceful sleep, she let her thoughts wander where they wanted. They seemed to have fixated upon a certain Jewish man with a short, dark beard and fiery brown eyes.

She sighed again, closing her eyes. Life would never again be the same for her.

&

Adonijah watched Anna tending to little Samah. Ramoth stood close by her side, his curious eyes following every move his mother made.

Feeling eyes upon him, Adonijah turned to Barak.

"You will be leaving for Jerusalem soon?" Barak asked.

Adonijah knew that wasn't what was on Barak's mind, but he was glad that his friend would defer to his desire to remain silent. He really didn't wish to discuss his thoughts with anyone at this time. His reluctance to do so was unsettling, because he and Barak had always shared their feelings with each other.

Adonijah observed the servants coming into the room to light the lamps. He hadn't realized that it had grown so late.

"Tomorrow," he answered Barak. "That will give me time in case anything untoward happens to delay us. I want to reach the city before Shavuot."

"Perhaps when you take the offering to the priest, you will see something of the famous Apostle Peter," Barak suggested. "I hear that he preaches in the synagogues every Sabbath, telling the Jews about Jesus."

"I'm certain that if I stay with Bithnia, I will. He has spoken at her house many times as well."

Anna came and sat beside her husband. She smiled when Adonijah instantly reached for the babe. Handing the child into his waiting arms, she told him, "I have missed worshiping with those in Jerusalem. It seems a long time since we have seen Aunt Bithnia, Pisgah, and Tamar."

Adonijah gently pushed aside the blanket cocooning Samah so that he could see her tiny face. He stroked her soft arms with one large finger. Suddenly he frowned, glancing up at Anna.

"You still refuse to put her in swaddling clothes? Aren't you afraid that her limbs will grow crooked?"

Nestling against Barak, Anna smiled. "I cannot bring myself to do so. At first, we couldn't do so because of her restricted breathing, but now. . ."

Ramoth climbed up next to his uncle. "What are swaddling clothes?"

Playing with children was one thing. Teaching them certain aspects of life was quite another. Adonijah turned from Ramoth's expectant face and beseeched Anna with his eyes. She only grinned.

"You started it. You explain."

Sighing, Adonijah turned back to Ramoth. "Swaddling clothes are what a baby is wrapped in to make certain that his limbs will grow straight."

Ramoth stared blankly at his uncle. Adonijah again turned to Anna. Shaking her head at Adonijah's reluctance to continue, she smiled wryly. "A baby is wrapped tightly in strips of cloth so that he is as straight as can be. That way his arms and legs will grow straight," she told her son.

Ramoth's voice was unyielding. "I wouldn't like that."

Barak, Anna, and Adonijah exchanged amused glances. Adonijah considered his nephew as the boy bounced around on the couch, his dancing brown eyes flitting from one adult to another. No, confining Ramoth would be like trying to wrestle with the wind. Anna spoke first.

"It has already been done to you, my son. It is done the first six months you are a babe."

Ramoth's eyebrows lifted as he digested this bit of information. His look went first to his sister, then followed a course down his own uniform body. The direction of his thoughts was clear when next he spoke.

"I'm glad my arms and legs are straight. Why isn't Samah wrapped in swaddling clothes?"

Anna threw Adonijah an exasperated look. "Now look what you've done."

Affronted, he held out his hands, shrugging his shoulders at the same time. "What?"

Disregarding him, Anna turned to her son. "At first, we

couldn't bind Samah because of her breathing problems."

"Is she six months old now?" the boy wanted to know.

Anna's eyes shot daggers at her husband when she heard him snicker. Rolling her eyes, she told Ramoth, "No, she isn't. But she has already grown and her limbs are still straight."

Ramoth's face clouded with confusion. "Then why use swaddling clothes?"

If looks could kill, Adonijah was certain he would be in his grave right about now. Trying to divert the young boy's attention, he lifted him from the couch and began twirling him above his head.

"Isn't it past your bedtime?"

"No!" Ramoth squealed when Adonijah threw him into the air.

"Yes," his mother disagreed, getting to her feet and waiting for Adonijah to set the boy back on his. Ramoth threw his father a pleading look. Barak grinned.

"You know that I don't dare argue with your mother."

Anna gave him a look that she usually reserved for Ramoth when he had driven her to distraction. Taking Ramoth by the hand, she exited the room, giving both Barak and Adonijah a disgusted look.

Adonijah, for one, could understand her pique. It wouldn't surprise him in the least if they found little Samah bundled in rags come morning, and Ramoth innocently explaining his desire to help.

Still grinning, Barak turned his attention to Adonijah.

"You've been spending quite a bit of time with Bilhah," he suggested.

Nonplused by the sudden change of topic, Adonijah was momentarily silenced. He ignored the implied question. It was not Bilhah that concerned Barak, of that he was certain.

"How were you able to reach her so quickly for the Lord, Barak? In less than a week's time you were able to convince her that Jesus was the Messiah."

Silently studying Adonijah, Barak took a moment to answer.

"Bilhah is a godly woman. She only wants to serve the Lord. It didn't take much to make her see the fulfillment of the scriptures in Jesus. Women tend to be much more receptive than men. I think it has to do with believing with the heart, as compared to believing with the mind."

Adonijah laid his head back against the couch, contemplating the ceiling. Closing his eyes, he lifted one dark eyebrow upwards. "Her granddaughter is not so. . .receptive."

Adonijah was tempted to confide in his friend. He had told Mara that he loved her, but did she understand that he only meant as a friend? At times he almost pitied her, but at others he grew irritated with her attitude. One minute he wanted to shake her until her teeth rattled, the next, he wanted to hold her close and comfort her like he would Ramoth.

Of course, there had never been a time when he held Ramoth that his stomach seemed to clench within him, his breathing becoming restricted. Mara seemed to incite such a reaction, and he wasn't quite certain why it was so. He had been around women before, both beautiful and not so beautiful, but none had ever affected him physically the way that Mara seemed to. It concerned him that this should be so.

"What time will you leave tomorrow?"

Adonijah dragged his gaze back to Barak. "The others will be ready at first light. They have decided to save themselves some money and not stop by a caravansary on the way. Since there will be such a great number of us, not to mention the dozens of others on the road headed for Jerusalem, they decided it would be safe enough to camp out in the open." Softly expelling his breath, Adonijah got reluctantly to his feet.

"I suppose I should get to bed. Tomorrow will be a long day."

Barak nodded. "I will see that Bilhah has a way to worship this Lord's day."

"Thank you."

Slapping his friend on the back, Adonijah left the room. He could hear Anna talking to Ramoth as he passed the boy's room. She was telling him a story about Moses. Stories of the great prophet were a favorite of Ramoth's, and he always wanted to hear one before he would go to sleep.

When Adonijah opened the door to his own room, he noticed that one of the servants had already lit the lamp. Darkness had fallen, and the shadows cast by the flame flickered in moving patterns about the room.

Going to the window, Adonijah studied the waxing moon. It would be full soon, and that boded well for the journey to Jerusalem. The night breeze was fresh with the scents of spring. Inhaling deeply, he thanked Jehovah for another day.

Blowing out the lamp, he crawled into bed, lying with his arms folded behind his head. Tomorrow he would leave for Jerusalem to give the Temple offering of two loaves of bread for the feast of Shavuot. He would be gone the better part of two weeks, which left him feeling uncommonly morose.

A lot could happen in two weeks. Closing his eyes, he began to fervently petition the Lord.

❧

Mara came up out of the water, her whole being flooded with joy. For the first time in her life, she felt clean all over—not just her body, but her soul as well.

When Barak had explained the need to be baptized into Christ, Mara had not hesitated. She had witnessed baptisms for years, though mainly from a distance. It was a required rite under Jewish custom for proselyte Gentiles to be baptized, and for the men, circumcised as well.

Still, she couldn't remember any person who had risen from the water with their face filled with joy. Surely her own face must look just such a way, because she felt so completely happy. The thought that her hair was hanging down her back in a dark brown wet mass, and that her face was available for all to see, did nothing to diminish her content.

Shivering, she moved towards the bank of the stream that fed the pool she had been immersed in. Although the sun was warm enough, the water was shaded by large sycamore trees.

Barak stepped out of the water with her, taking the opportunity to give her a gentle hug. Anna did the same, tears shimmering in her eyes.

"Welcome, little sister," she said.

"Oh, Anna," Mara breathed. "I feel so. . .alive!"

Wrapping Mara in a large linen towel, Anna returned her smile. "You are. Alive to Christ. Dead to sin."

Mara turned to her grandmother. There was understanding in the old faded eyes staring back at her. Yes, Grandmother would appreciate what she was feeling. The two hugged, tears of happiness on both of their faces. No words needed to be exchanged.

"Come," Barak told them, drying his legs beneath his short white tunic. "Come back to the villa and we will celebrate."

Mara was reluctant. Only with Barak's assurances that it would be only they, and with her grandmother's prodding, was she finally persuaded to go. In the end, she was glad that she went. It had been a long time since she had been able to play with little Samah. Even Ramoth was on his best behavior for the occasion, for which his mother was thoroughly grateful.

Anna sat next to Mara on the couch in the triclinium, casting a motherly eye over her daughter.

"She is a good baby," Mara told her softly.

Anna nodded. "Yes, she is that. I'm afraid we spoil her, Barak, Ramoth, Adonijah, and I."

Mara was tickling Samah's palm with her thumb. "She deserves to be spoilt."

"Well, deserving or not, she gets it." Anna grew somber. "Life will be hard enough for her in time."

Mara silently agreed. Still, although pitied by others, at least Samah wouldn't be shunned. Blamed for every misfortune that hit a village.

"Adonijah should return soon," Anna told her, watching with interest the color that flooded into Mara's cheeks.

After a long period of silence, Mara finally asked, "Have you heard from him?"

"No, we haven't, but the grape harvesting has begun. He will want to be here for that."

Since she was busy with the baby, Mara didn't see the look Anna exchanged with her husband and his almost imperceptible nod in Mara's direction.

"Mara," Anna began, and Mara was surprised at the hesitation in her voice. She gave Anna her full attention.

"Yes?"

Once again Anna glanced at her husband. Mara's brows drew together as she waited for her friend to continue. Anna's face was solemn when she turned back to Mara.

"Barak and I have something we would like to ask you. A favor, if you will."

There was something very serious in Anna's normally cheerful eyes. One thing Mara knew for certain. Whatever these people wanted of her, if it was in her power, she would gladly do it for them. She told Anna so.

Still, Anna seemed reluctant. Finally gathering her courage, Anna pulled back the covering from Samah's little face. The babe's eyes were closed, her rosebud mouth slightly puckered. Anna watched her daughter instead of Mara.

"It has to do with Samah."

"I would do anything for Samah," Mara interrupted.

Anna met her eyes, and smiled. "I had hoped you would say so. You see, Ramoth needs so much of my attention that at times I feel that I'm neglecting my daughter. Ramoth has to be watched very closely."

Mara could certainly understand that. The boy was never out of mischief. The problem was, he was never mean, nor did he intentionally get himself into trouble. It just seemed to follow him wherever he went.

"Anyway," Anna continued, "I would feel much better if there were someone here to help me keep an eye on Samah when I have to tend to Ramoth."

"But what has that to do with me? You have plenty of servants for such a task."

For a moment, Anna was silent. When her eyes connected with Mara's, Mara could see the distress lurking in their depths.

"It's true that we have plenty of servants, and while we know they could be trusted to care for Samah, they do not. . . do not love her the way that you do."

Understanding filled Mara's features. It was the same everywhere. People always seemed to shy away from disabilities, as though people who had them were less than human. Or as though they were afraid they might catch it, like some disease.

"You want me to come to the villa each day to care for Samah?"

Anna shook her head. "No. We. . .we want you to come to the villa to live. You and Bilhah."

Stunned, Mara sat blinking at Anna. She was bereft of speech. What would her grandmother say to such a thing? And could she, Mara, bring herself to live in a houseful of people who would constantly see her deformity? And what if something bad happened to Anna, Ramoth, or the babe? Would Barak then blame her?

As though reading her mind, Anna lay her hand across Mara's arm. "Barak and I have prayed long and hard about what to do with Samah. We believe you just might be the answer to those prayers."

"Me?" Mara somehow doubted that she could be the answer to anyone's prayers.

"Yes."

There was no doubting the sincerity of Anna's belief, but as a new Christian, Mara had a long way to go before she had the faith Anna had. Did Jehovah really care that Anna and Barak needed help with their daughter? Was it possible that He had arranged things so that they all fulfilled a mutual need?

Mara's first instinct was to refuse. For twenty years she had shied away from the world, and now she would be thrust into it with a vengeance. She glanced across to where her grandmother was in conversation with Barak. Although she still retained that look of peace, her age was telling on her. Her thinness spoke of days without proper nourishment. If they came here, they would never go hungry again. Grandmother deserved that, after all the years she had spent going without for Mara's benefit. Now was no time to be selfish.

"I will have to speak to my grandmother."

A relieved expression crossed Anna's face. "Of course."

Mara wavered. "Are you certain of this?"

"I am *very* certain," Anna told her firmly.

Anna got up and crossed to Bilhah. She said something that sent the old woman's look Mara's way. Nodding, Bilhah came and sat down next to Mara.

"Anna says that you have something you wish to speak to me about."

Surprisingly to Mara, her grandmother readily agreed. By nightfall, their few belongings had been brought from the hut, and Mara found herself ensconced in a beautiful bedroom. There were two beds in it, one for Mara, and one for her grandmother. This pleased Mara, for it had been many years since she had slept without the old woman.

When they joined the family at the table for the evening meal, Mara rejoiced at her good fortune. Her heart was full to bursting. A new spirit, and a new life—could anyone ask for more?

She watched her grandmother as she reclined next to Anna. They were deep in discussion, so neither was aware of her scrutiny. The tired lines of her grandmother's face had lessened considerably, and it occurred to Mara that she had been the cause of much of her grandmother's concern.

Bilhah seemed more content. She had said an odd thing earlier that Mara had been unable to puzzle out or forget.

"Now, you will be taken care of."

There had been a wealth of satisfaction in her voice. When Mara had asked her meaning, her grandmother had merely shrugged and told her not to mind an old woman's rambling.

An odd premonition settled around Mara like a shroud as she watched her grandmother's animated face. She and Anna were discussing Heaven, and the words of Jesus concerning a mansion there.

Mara frowned. It was almost as though Grandmother were eager to get there. A mansion in heaven would be wonderful, Mara decided, but only if they could share it together. Even the rudest hut had seemed heavenly when she had shared it with her grandmother. Life without her grandmother was not to be contemplated.

Mara reflected on these thoughts several times over the next few days. They had almost become an obsession with her, causing her to watch her grandmother more carefully. Only when she was with little Samah did the feeling of impending doom lessen.

For that reason, it came as no surprise when Mara awoke one bright, sunny morning and found her grandmother had died in her sleep.

seven

The sirocco had hit with an intensity that left Adonijah breathless. His caravan had been caught halfway between Jerusalem and Sychar, and there was little to protect them from the driving, cold, east wind.

Since most siroccos lasted about three days, he decided to hunker down against the large rock that he had stumbled over during the storm, and make himself as comfortable as possible until some of the others had erected some form of shelter for themselves. Visibility was so poor that those trying to erect shelter continually collided with each other, and he could hear their angry voices above the howling wind.

After several long minutes that seemed more like hours, Adonijah decided that comfort was an impossibility.

Peering out from the confines of the burnous he had borrowed from a man in the caravan, Adonijah could barely make out the figures of the huddling animals, their tails turned towards the east, their heads hanging close to the ground. They were a pitiful sight. Squinting his eyes, the only part of his body exposed by the dark cloak, Adonijah decided that they looked pretty much as he felt.

A fine, yellowish dust haze filled the air, discoloring the landscape, and generally causing discomfort for everyone.

Although the wind itself blew cold, temperatures were already rising around him. That was the strangeness of the siroccos. As the air became warmer, it also became much dryer, and Adonijah could feel the dryness closing his throat.

Pulling his water skin from beneath his cloak, he took a swig of the water and swirled it around in his mouth. Grit filled his nostrils and clung to his teeth.

Finally, he deemed it safe to emerge from his semi-shelter and put up his own small tent. Before he was even finished, the black goatskin was taking on a yellow hue.

Crawling beneath his haven, he prepared himself to wait out the storm. Patience was not one of his finer virtues, especially when he had had a prodding all day long to get back to Sychar as quickly as possible.

Worry furrowed a gash between his eyebrows. Faces of his loved ones kept floating before his eyes. Anna. Barak. Ramoth. Samah. One replaced by another.

Suddenly, there came a picture of Mara, her brown eyes clouded by distress. He felt his stomach give a sudden lurch. In such a short time the woman had found a place in his heart right along with the others. She needed a friend so badly, and advisable or not, he wanted to be that friend.

But if all he felt was friendship, why then did he feel his blood thunder through his veins every time he remembered holding her close?

❧

Mara bent close to her grandmother's body, pressing her own warm lips against Bilhah's cold ones in the age-old custom of the Jews. She would be considered unclean for seven days, but then so would the others who were helping her prepare the body.

Although custom also dictated a seven-day mourning period, Mara knew her time of grieving would go on for much longer. All day she had struggled desperately to hold back the tears.

Anna came to her now, placing an arm around her waist, her hazel eyes filled with compassion. The tears that had threatened before now came in a raging torrent.

Mara clung to Anna, barely registering the other woman's soothing words.

"No words can lift your grief, Mara. I know that. But I want you to know that Jesus has prepared a place for Bilhah, and she has gone to be with Him."

"I know."

Anna had to bend close to hear the softly spoken, grief-ravaged words. She patted Mara's back, as she had often done for little Samah.

"Come. We must prepare the body. The men will be here soon to carry the bier."

Mara had to push her feelings aside in order to get through this time. The climate in the Palestinian region didn't allow for delay in burying a loved one's body. Within twenty-four hours, it would begin to decompose.

Besides, it was better if she handled the preparations herself; then she would know that Grandmother was being cared for by loving hands. She glanced up at Anna, who was gently washing Bilhah's arms as Mara washed the legs.

Anna was a good woman. Mara didn't mind that Anna's hands were on her grandmother, for every touch spoke of love. Anna and Bilhah had grown to appreciate each other very much over the short period of time they had known each other.

Taking the flask of scented oil, Anna poured some into her own hands and then handed Mara the bottle. The aromatic scent of myrrh and balsam filled the air. Had it not been for Barak and Anna's generosity, Mara would have had to make do with a much cheaper fragrance, if any at all. Each moment, Mara felt her indebtedness to the couple grow.

Anna began wrapping the hands with strips of linen, and Mara did the same with the feet. As they wrapped, they sprinkled fragrant spices between the strips, another extravagance Mara would have had to do without.

Finally the body was wrapped and all that was left was the cloth to be placed around the face. Anna stood back and allowed Mara to do that part on her own.

Mara stood for a moment looking down on the beloved, wrinkled face. Softly, she stroked her fingers over the delicate features.

"Good-bye, Grandmother. I love you." She closed her own eyes, and in a voice husky with tears, she petitioned the Lord. "Please, Jesus. Take care of her."

After covering her grandmother's face, Mara removed from her own body the colorful linen tunic that Anna had given her several days earlier. Lifting a sackcloth from the chair beside the bed, Mara dropped it over her head. The rough flax material scratched as it slid down her body, but she paid it little heed.

Going to the brazier in the corner of the room, she scooped a handful of ashes and began rubbing them on her face and arms. The soot soon veiled the uncovered portions of her body, somewhat concealing her deformity.

Since Anna had gone to see about the funeral litter, Mara sat down to think. What was to become of her now? She couldn't continue living here with Anna and Barak. She had always hated charity, and the only reason she had accepted it from them was for her grandmother's sake. Anna may have tried to make Mara believe that she was being helpful, but Mara recognized the tactic. No matter what they said, they were offering her a place to stay when she had no right.

Perhaps they did believe that they owed her their son's life, but if she hadn't been skulking in the dark around the threshing floor, the child would probably never have been so far from the camp in the first place.

Impatient with her thoughts, she went to the window and looked outside. The bright sunlight and chittering birds lent a gaiety to the atmosphere that she was far from feeling. This day should be dark and gloomy, and yet, if what Barak and Adonijah had told her was true, it was really a day of celebration. Jesus had overcome death, and now Grandmother would live with Him forever.

A choked sob escaped her throat. Turning back to the room, she was taken aback to see Adonijah standing in the doorway. He was covered with a fine layer of yellow dust, his face peering out at her from the confines of a black burnous. His sympathetic eyes were fixed intently on her. For a brief moment, Mara felt an overwhelming joy at seeing him again. She wanted nothing more than to run to his arms and feel again the safety she had felt before when his strong embrace had held her close. She took several steps forward, and then stopped.

Since she didn't attempt any further movement, Adonijah started to go to her instead, but she quickly held up a hand to stop him.

"Don't come any closer. You might accidentally touch me, and I am unclean."

Adonijah frowned as she cowered away from him. She looked so small and helpless in her sackcloth dress, the blackness of the ashes on her face making her eyes seem even larger than before. If she hadn't warned him, he would surely have taken her in his arms to give her comfort. Even now the inclination to do so was very strong. Her brown eyes were dulled by grief, their normal vibrancy gone for the moment.

"I'm sorry I wasn't here when Bilhah. . .when you needed me. We were held up."

Mara turned away, brushing at the returning tears leaving paths through the ashes on her cheeks. "It's all right. You couldn't have known."

As he studied her, Adonijah felt again the strange stirrings within him. He still wasn't quite certain what to do about them. It was becoming much harder to dislodge the woman from his mind. Jehovah was trying to tell him something, but what? Suddenly, he was tongue-tied, not knowing what else to say.

"It is time," he finally told her softly.

She nodded, going carefully past him until she reached the door. She glanced back once, and the yearning in her eyes was almost his undoing.

"I am glad you made it back in time," she told him, her voice torn by heartache.

"As am I."

Adonijah watched her leave, his feelings warring within himself. He had always hated to see anything, or anyone, hurt. Often, he had cuddled Ramoth after one of the boy's frequent "accidents." Now, he wanted to do the same for Mara. The difference was, thoughts of Ramoth didn't stir his blood. The fact that Mara did caused him no end of irritation. Pity was no substitute for true friendship, and anything less would be wrong. Anything more was impossible, regardless of what Mara's grandmother had suggested to him.

Thoughts of Bilhah warmed his heart. The old lady had been to him the grandmother he had never had. In the short time he had known her, he had loved her. Often they had spoken of Heaven and the Lord's return, but that wasn't her only concern. They had conversed many hours about her troubled granddaughter. Bilhah was wise, and besides loving her, Adonijah had respected her.

He glanced at the wrapped body awaiting the litter. There was something he must do before they carried the body away.

❧

Mara took her place behind the funeral bier and waited for the men to lift the litter to their shoulders. She was surprised to see among those present that one man was clean shaven, designating him as a true mourner. Since the other men had been paid by Barak to carry the litter, they didn't feel compelled to show true mourning.

It took Mara a moment to recognize the man, never having seen him without his beard, but those brown eyes could only belong to one person. Only Adonijah's look had ever made her feel the way those eyes were making her feel.

She turned away from that piercing gaze now, and found Anna beside her. Barak stood just behind her, and he, too, was clean shaven. He strode forward and took his place behind Adonijah. Realizing the depth of their esteem, Mara felt the tears threatening again.

Mara's misty eyes met Anna's, and Anna smiled slightly. "Barak wanted to show his love and respect. I suspect Adonijah felt the same."

A solid lump lodged in Mara's throat and she couldn't have spoken even if she had wanted to. Such love as these people had shown her family certainly set them apart from others. No wonder Bilhah had so quickly believed that the Messiah had come. Only power from Jehovah could change the hatred and fear she had encountered all her life. For the first time since she had awakened this morning and found her grandmother gone, Mara felt a true measure of peace.

Another way that Barak had shown his love for Bilhah was the number of professional mourners he had hired. The law required that even the poor must have at least one, but Barak had hired six. His willingness to go to that expense touched Mara deeply.

The hired women followed the litter, their loud wails accompanied by the thrumming tambourines and flutes. As the procession moved along the streets, other people joined the retinue.

The professional mourners moved among the crowd, swaying back and forth in a kind of melancholy dance, and with consummate acting skills, they were able to bring many to genuine grief.

They called out to others, speaking in terms of love and

tenderness about Bilhah. Although it was a custom, and would prove to others that Grandmother was loved, Mara cringed at their hollow words. How could they speak of loving Grandmother that way when they didn't even know her? It all seemed so deceitful, somehow. She prayed again for strength from Jehovah to get her through this difficult time.

When they arrived at the plot of land to the east of the village used for burying the dead, the entourage stopped. Barak had offered to give Bilhah a cave for her tomb, but Mara had refused. When the time came, she hoped to lie next to her grandmother in this little plot of earth.

Until that time, she would take great care to see that it was kept whitewashed. Jesus had spoken of those who were like tombs where the whitewashing had been neglected. Other people would become defiled unknowingly merely by stepping over them. Well, she would make certain that no one became defiled by her pure, sweet grandmother.

The wails and moans of those around her scarcely disturbed Mara's thoughts. She knew that others were looking at her askance, but how could she lament when although her heart was riven with sorrow, it was also filled with joy? Her grandmother was with the Lord. In her mind, those words kept time to the pounding of the funeral drum in the village.

With the Lord. With the Lord. Over and over the refrain beat through her mind.

Barak's voice quoted from the Psalms of King David. "Precious in the sight of the Lord is the death of His saints."

She was glad for her grandmother, but the persistent thought that she herself was now alone left her feeling more dejected by the minute. Why had Jehovah taken Grandmother and left her behind? If she allowed her thoughts to wander, all she could see was an unending future of dismal days spent gleaning the fields for her sustenance, and that all by herself.

It was the aloneness that terrified her more than anything. Fear, hatred, rejection—she could face it all, but not alone. Never alone.

The frightening future loomed before her until her body trembled with dread. The horror of it became overwhelming, and finally, not able to stand it a moment longer, she lifted her eyes to the sky and moaned, "Lord, Jesus. Please, take me too!"

❧

Mara opened her eyes to find Anna bending over her, wiping her face with a wet cloth.

"What happened?" Glancing around the room, she realized that she was back at the villa. "How did I get here?"

Anna smiled wryly. "You fainted, and unclean or not, Adonijah brought you home."

Mara sat up slowly, placing a hand against her forehead when the room began to tilt around her. "I'm sorry."

Clicking her tongue, Anna helped her to sit. "You have nothing to apologize for. It could happen to anyone." She smiled fully. "And probably has."

Mara dropped her eyes to the floor. "I meant that I was sorry for embarrassing you."

Anna took one of Mara's hands and squeezed gently, her hazel eyes sparking indignantly. "How could we be embarrassed by your honest grief? No, Mara, never that. Besides, you have had nothing to eat since last night. With the heat and your grief, it's to be expected."

There was a tap on the door and Adonijah stood in the open portal. His eyes were on Mara, but he spoke to Anna.

"The neighbors have brought some food."

Mara lifted her eyes to Anna. "I'm sorry for that, too."

"Don't be foolish," Anna scoffed. "The house may be considered unclean because your grandmother died here, but I wouldn't have it any other way. So we can't cook in the house for seven days, so what?" Her voice softened. "We loved her, too, Mara. We wouldn't have wanted her to be anywhere else."

Mara dropped her gaze to the floor again, nodding her head. She didn't realize that Anna had left the room until Adonijah came and sat next to her.

Mara turned to say something to him, but her words dried up as she noticed again his clean-shaven face. Adonijah rubbed at his jaw, a half smile curving up the right side of his mouth. Mara could tell that he was embarrassed. No Jewish man would be caught dead without his beard, except in the case of mourning. Again, Mara was awed at the concern he showed for a woman he barely knew.

Reaching up, she let her fingers graze his jaw, marveling at the soft texture of his skin. What had been hidden beneath the close cut of his beard was now visible. As she had suspected, he had a firm, square jaw. Stubborn, she would call it.

"Do I dare tell you that I like you better without your beard?"

One dark brow winged its way upward in disbelief. "Surely not."

She couldn't help it; she had to grin at his affronted voice. "It makes you no less a man, Adonijah."

Adonijah was no more startled by the huskily spoken words than Mara herself was. Blushing furiously, she dropped her hands and turned quickly away.

Adonijah saw the color creep into her cheeks and understood her embarrassment all too well. He was feeling a bit that way himself, although the timbre of Mara's voice had sent the warmth flooding through his body. He tried to consider what he must look like to her with a bare face, and failed.

Except for cases of mourning, it was considered unmanly to be clean shaven—even more so now since it was the

Roman way to have hairless faces. Jews took pride in their distinctiveness.

But it was more than that causing his chagrin. Her words had given a strange boost to his ego. It pleased him that Mara saw him as a man. Still, he wasn't quite certain what to say to relieve both of them of their disquiet.

It was Mara who broke the silence. "I must go back to the poor community."

Adonijah's eyes instantly darkened with anger. "Never. You belong here now."

She shook her head, still refusing to meet his eyes. "No, Adonijah. I cannot stay."

Adonijah tried to curb the rising displeasure her words had caused. To argue with the woman would only seal her fate as surely as Roman cement sealed a wall. Trying to keep the censure out of his voice, he told her, "Surely that can wait until after your seven days of mourning."

"It would be better for me to go now."

Throwing all caution to the wind, Adonijah took her chin in an unyielding grip, turning her to face him. Mara quailed beneath the fury she saw flashing in his eyes.

"You would do that to Anna and Barak? Have you no consideration for their feelings? They cared for Bilhah, too. To leave now would be like a slap in the face."

"I—I didn't think it would matter so much."

"We shall see," he told her inflexibly. Getting up, he quickly exited the room, only to return a few moments later followed by Anna and Barak.

"Mara, is it true?"

There was no denying the distress filling Anna's features as she hurried across the room. It was obvious that Barak was no less concerned.

Adonijah stood behind them, feet planted firmly apart, arms crossed over his chest. He reminded Mara of a Roman statue, except that his eyes were glitteringly alive.

Mara's gaze returned to Anna. "I can't stay. You have all been very kind, but I–I can't stay."

Anna seated herself beside Mara on the bed. "But why? We love having you here. You're like a part of our family now."

"But I'm not!"

Three pairs of eyebrows lifted at her vehement declaration.

"I'm sorry. I don't mean to offend." She picked at the rough cloth of her tunic, her eyes cast to the ground.

"Mara. . ." Anna turned to her husband helplessly. He knelt before Mara and lifted her chin until he could see her eyes.

"We want you here. Samah and Ramoth want you here." His eyes flicked briefly to Adonijah. "Even Adonijah wants you to stay."

Mara ignored Adonijah, focusing her attention instead on Anna and Barak. "I can't stay."

Barak's eyes met his wife's, and he shrugged. There was really nothing they could do if Mara had decided.

"Will you at least stay until your seven days of mourning are finished?" Anna pleaded. "Then you and I can go through the ritual ceremony together to relieve us of our uncleanness."

Mara glanced briefly at Adonijah. Although he said nothing, his eyes were boring holes through her. It made her angry that he could make her feel lower than an asp, as though she were committing some vile sin. Her own eyes sparked with resolve.

"I will stay until then."

Sighing with relief, Anna motioned for the others to leave the room. "Mara needs some rest."

Although Adonijah did as he was bid, he was reluctant. He followed Anna to the door, glancing once at Mara. In his mind, things were not yet settled. Someone had to make the woman listen to reason, and it looked like the job fell to him. Surely Mara hadn't become a part of their lives just to disappear now.

He was filled with sudden anxiety when he remembered her in the grain fields, and the other people's reaction to her. What would life be like for her without Bilhah?

Mara watched with relief as they moved out of the room. She could faintly discern Anna's words as the men followed her.

"We must pray."

٭

Mara rolled the sackcloth into a ball and laid it on the bed beside her old, frayed dress. She donned instead the blue linen tunic that Anna had given her earlier. She would be going home today, but she wouldn't for the world hurt Anna any further by rejecting her gift.

Ordinarily, their hut would have been occupied by now, but it would seem that Mara's reputation had followed her. No one was willing to chance becoming cursed by staying in the same house that Mara had lived in. Since it was still empty, she could return any time she wished. The thought depressed her.

Adonijah met her at the foot of the stairs, taking the roll of clothing from her unresisting fingers.

"I would like to talk to you a moment," he told her.

"What about?"

Instead of answering, he wrapped his fingers around her forearm and pulled her with him to the peristyle. The morning sun shone down brightly, though it was still fairly cool in the garden. Adonijah led her to a stone bench beneath a gnarled fig tree, seating himself beside her.

Mara waited for him to speak, watching in fascination as the color came and went in his face. The dark hair returning to his chin and cheeks gave him a somewhat rakish air. He could have been a brigand, although there was no denying that he was a handsome one. Mara felt again the now familiar quickstepping of her heartbeats at his nearness.

"You wished to say something?"

Lifting his eyes to the heavens, Adonijah took a deep breath. He opened his lips several times to speak, and each time he couldn't find the words he wanted to say. Finally, he told her, "We still don't want you to leave."

Disheartened, Mara sighed. For one insane moment she had thought that Adonijah was going to say something on his own behalf. Instead, he spoke for Anna and Barak, although he included himself as well. They still believed they owed her for Ramoth's life.

"I have already told you, I can't stay. It wouldn't be right."

Irritated, Adonijah glared at her. "What wouldn't be right about it? We all. . .we all care about you. As Anna said, you are like one of the family."

"But I'm not, Adonijah. I'm *not* one of the family." She thought for a moment. "Perhaps I could be a servant?"

The look Adonijah bestowed on her could have blistered the feathers from a dove.

"There is nothing wrong with being a servant," she told him in vexation.

"Anna and Barak have enough servants. They don't need any more."

"Well, then," Mara reasoned. "There's nothing more to say, is there?"

She got to her feet, but he quickly jerked her back down. Angry eyes met angry eyes.

"Listen to me a moment," Adonijah beseeched her, his teeth clenched. Mara closed her mouth on the angry torrent of words begging for release.

"Is this going to be another conversation like those from this past week?" she asked him heavily. "Because if it is, I really don't want to go through this again."

Adonijah considered the times he had talked with her over the last several days. Each time he tried to talk her into staying, he had the feeling that he was arguing with a cedar from Lebanon. "You are an unreasonable woman!" he told her.

"*I'm* unreasonable. You are the one who won't listen to reason!"

Sighing, Adonijah laid a restraining finger across her lips. "Will you listen to me?" When Mara subsided, he continued.

"You are my friend, and I care for you."

Mara opened her mouth to respond, but quickly closed it at his quelling look.

"I don't want to see you go back to a life of poverty," he continued. "The thought bothers me, Mara. Maybe more than I can make you understand. You saved Ramoth's life. You've helped little Samah to feel loved. . ."

He didn't know how to continue. Words seemed inadequate. Mara laid a hand against his forearm, and Adonijah's eyes widened as he felt a flash like fire course through his body. Mara must have been feeling much of the same, for she jerked her hand away as though it had been burned. For a moment their eyes were locked together, but Mara quickly looked away.

"You have all been good to me. I. . .I love all of you. I couldn't ask for better friends, but. . .but I would feel like a beggar if I stayed."

Adonijah said nothing for a long time. Finally, he sighed and turned back to her. Although his face was as white as the marble fountain in the center of the garden, his brown eyes burned with life.

"Would you still feel so if you married me?"

eight

Mara dropped the half-filled grain bag to the table, staring at it absently. Her mind was busy replaying the scene that had just occurred in the barley fields of the man named Jehu. Jehu's manager had noticed Mara among the gleaners and had angrily expelled her from the field.

It would seem word of Barak's misfortunes had spread among the community of Sychar, and as usual, the blame had landed squarely at Mara's unfortunate feet.

Before, she would have been angry and wanted to seek revenge—if not overtly, then at least in her prayers to the Almighty. Now, she felt only the hurt and humiliation. Only the vivid picture of Jesus hanging on a wooden cross had stayed her fiery temper. For every sin she committed, she could imagine the nails being driven deeper into the flesh of His palms. She shivered, sliding into the chair beside the table.

She was struggling, that much was certain. Anna had warned her that this would be so. She belonged to Jesus now, and Satan would attack her unmercifully while her faith was still shallow. Anna had shared one of the Lord's parables with her about a farmer scattering seed. The birds ate some, the thorns choked some, and some grew and died among the rocks. Mara wanted to be one of the strong ones that fell among good soil and produced fruit. She didn't want to fall back into despair after finding such peace and joy.

Pulling the bowl used for grinding grain towards her, Mara began to shed the barley kernels into it. When she was finished, she realized that there would be only enough for a small loaf of bread, barely enough to satisfy her gnawing hunger. Not for the first time, she thanked Jehovah for taking her grandmother from this life and sparing her any more worries. Grandmother had died happy, thinking that Mara would be well cared for. It would have been true, too, except for Mara's stubborn pride.

Her stomach rumbled, sounding like thunder in the quietness of the hut. She was so hungry. For three weeks now she had sustained herself with the little gleanings she had been able to procure from the harvests around her—sometimes wheat, sometimes barley, sometimes grapes and other fruits. It had been enough to keep her alive, but barely. If she had been willing to humble her pride, she could have gone to Anna and Barak and they would have offered her food, but she just couldn't bring herself to do it.

As she had feared at her grandmother's funeral, the solitude was fast getting to her. She had always considered herself a loner, but now she realized that she had only been fooling herself. Grandmother had always been there to fill her need for companionship. There had never been a time when she had been truly alone. Until now.

If she closed her eyes, she could pretend that Grandmother was sitting in the hut, her raspy voice lifted in praise to Jehovah. The echoes of a favorite psalm whispered softly through the interior of her mind. A small smile slowly curled her lips while tears ran silently down her cheeks.

"Mara."

She jumped, almost convinced that her thoughts had conjured her grandmother's spirit. Eyes flying open, she whirled to find Adonijah standing in the doorway.

"Adonijah! You frightened me."

His brown eyes regarded her coldly. He said nothing as his look swiftly scanned her from head to foot. Noticing the tears on her face, his eyes softened slightly. "Why are you crying?"

He came into the hut, dumping a bag on the table. If he noticed the sparseness of her meal, he said nothing. He stood resolutely beside her chair, waiting for her explanation.

"I. . .it's nothing. I was feeling a little lonely, I suppose."

Adonijah's lips tightened into a thin line, but he refrained from comment. He could have reminded her that her loneliness was her own doing, but he stifled the impulse. "Anna sent you some things. She said to tell you that she hopes things are well with you."

Mara dropped her gaze to the table, nervously moving the bowl of barley from side to side with her hands. She felt at a decided disadvantage with Adonijah towering over her, his displeasure evident. She hadn't seen him since that day more than three weeks ago when he had shocked her with his bizarre marriage proposal. When he had offered to marry her, she had at first been excited, but then reality had quickly set in. She was certain that he still felt he owed her for Ramoth's life.

She had turned him down in a voice that left no room for argument. At the hurt look in his eyes, she had almost relented, but pity and duty were no basis for a marriage. How could she ever hope to explain that to him and make him understand? His character was such that he would always fulfill his obligations.

Adonijah watched the emotions play across her features. She looked so like a wounded dove, those brown eyes full of confusion, that he wanted to reach out and take her into his arms to comfort her. Why was it he always felt the need to console her? Hadn't she made it plain that he wasn't needed, or wanted? His own pride had been dented considerably by her refusal of his offer of marriage. He should leave it alone, but somehow he just couldn't.

"I want to know why you are crying, Mara," he told her inflexibly. "It's more than loneliness, I believe." He pointed to the meager contents of the bowl. "Is this all you have to eat?"

She glanced at his face, and quickly looked away. "I. . .I wasn't able to finish gleaning in the fields today."

"Why?"

The word came out with the force of an arrow flying from a bow. Mara shrugged her shoulders. "Th–the manager asked me to leave the field."

Adonijah's swift intake of breath spoke of his quickly fired anger. "Who? Who asked you to leave?"

Sensing his rising fury, Mara hastened to try to soothe him. "It is of no concern, Adonijah. What is done, is done."

His eyes locked with hers and refused to let go. "Whose field were you in?"

Mara knew that he expected an answer. She recognized the stubborn set of that chin. "I was in the field of a man named Jehu. I do not know the manager's name."

Adonijah's gaze had gone to the window as though he could see to the fields they were discussing. His look returned to Mara. "Jared," he told her. "I will talk to him."

Mara placed a hand over his where it clenched the table. "Please don't. It doesn't matter."

Adonijah's look rested on their coupled hands before lifting again to Mara's distressed features. Slowly, he slid into the seat opposite her at the table. A tick worked convulsively in his cheek as he clenched his teeth together to keep from spilling the angry words begging for release.

"Why won't you marry me?" he finally demanded. "Then all of this would be taken care of."

Mara turned away from his searching eyes. Oh, how she longed to take him up on his offer. She had thought of little else for the past three weeks. She certainly had enough love to give; she thought that she could make him happy, but could she really? Would he be ashamed to be seen with a woman with a deformed face?

"Adonijah, when you marry, it won't be to someone like me," she told him softly. "You will marry someone beautiful, and whole—"

He jumped to his feet, his hands clenching at his sides. He began to pace like a caged lion, making the hut appear even smaller than before. "Thunder! You make me so angry at times I want to wring your little neck!"

Mara could see that he meant it. Her eyes went wide as he silently struggled for self-control. She had seen him angry before, but never like this. He had certainly worked himself into a fine frenzy. She fervently prayed that he could, indeed, contain his wrath.

Seeing her distress, Adonijah took a deep breath, firmly reining in his rising fury. He was frightening Mara, he could see that, but it was not with her alone that he was angry. He was sorely tempted to seek Jared out in Jehu's fields and give the man a throttling he wouldn't soon forget.

Calming himself, he knelt beside Mara's chair, placing one hand on the back, his other on the table before her. Without realizing it, he was surrounding her with his protection.

"Mara," he sighed, "I have told you before that there is more to life than beauty. If when I fought the lioness her claws had raked my face until it was deformed, would I be any less your friend?"

The picture he invoked made Mara's skin rise in bumps. Even the thought of Adonijah beneath the she-cat's claws was enough to make her heart lurch within her. If something happened to mar his physical perfection, would Mara love him less? No. That was not possible.

She focused on her hands twisting the frayed belt of her tunic. For her life, she could not look Adonijah in the face.

"People should marry for love," she whispered, not answering his question.

Adonijah bent close to hear the soft words. He smiled

slightly, noting the indecision in her voice. For the first time, he felt hope that she might reconsider her earlier rejection of him. It had become an obsession with him to have her for his wife. He could no more explain it than he could deny it. "How many people do you know who do so?"

"Anna and Barak."

"They are unique," he answered just as softly. "Barak's parents didn't marry for love, but they found it together." He took one of her hands and held it. "We are more fortunate than most, because we already have friendship, and the common bond of our Lord." He tilted her chin until he could see her eyes. "There is already love there, Mara. We only have to let it grow."

For a long moment Mara said nothing, only stared into his solemn eyes. There was anguish in her voice when she next spoke.

"But I'm cursed."

Adonijah realized that this was the center of the problem. How often had she heard those words, and how often had those piercing darts wounded her soul? Could he help her forget? He wanted so badly to do so, but he wasn't certain he knew just how to go about it. He stood, pulling her up into his arms. He held her tightly while she sobbed against his chest. He rocked her gently, allowing her to spill her grief.

"You little infant, don't be foolish. Jehovah loves you enough to have allowed His son to die for you. Would He then curse you?"

As the words soaked into her mind, her sobbing ceased. Once again she could hear the whispered voice of her dreams calling out to her. Lifting tear-drenched eyes to Adonijah's face, Mara's lips parted in silent awe. What Adonijah said was true. Jehovah had not cursed her; only her own weak mind and the even weaker minds of others had made her believe so.

"I will shame you," she told him harshly.

He shook his head. "Never. Believe me when I tell you this."

Mara searched his face for any flame of emotion, but could find not even a flicker. "You will want children."

One dark brow lifted upwards, his lips curling without humor. Mara's cheeks darkened with color. She pushed out of his arms, turning her back on him.

Adonijah studied her as she shrank away from him. She was thin to the point of emaciation. Her clothes were clean, but ragged. Still, if not for the mark on her face, she would have rivaled the fairest in the land for beauty. Far from being repelled by what he saw, he was drawn like a moth to flame. Even more importantly, he could see beyond her physical characteristics to the beauty of her soul. She was so full of love it lighted her entire being. In this way, she reminded him of Anna. His hands settled warmly on her shoulders.

"In time. We have plenty of time to think about such things as children. Let us be content for the time being to get to know each other."

Mara felt herself faltering. "But what if you find someone else to love?"

He turned her around to face him, forcing her chin up until he could see her face. "You should know me better than that, Mara."

She could tell he was growing exasperated with her. She wanted so much to agree to his terms of a companionship marriage, but she also longed to be loved as a woman. Could she survive a marriage of friendship when her feelings for Adonijah were so intense? Even now, his touch made her yearn for more. Would he ever be able to overcome his aversion to her deformity and allow them to have a physical relationship like normal couples? As though he could read her thoughts, he bent and touched his lips briefly to hers.

Only an instant did lips touch lips, yet that brief contact

seared Mara as deeply as a smith's iron. She lifted startled eyes to Adonijah and found him staring at her, his face full of wonder. Slowly, he lowered his mouth back to hers. His lips moved over hers, his hands sliding across her back until she was molded close. For an eon of time they clung together until Mara felt faint from the contact. Her head reeled giddily when Adonijah released her. Though his breathing was as ragged as hers, he said nothing, moving away from her to stare out the door. She sank unsteadily back into the chair.

She saw Adonijah's hands clench into fists at his side, while her own shook so badly she pulled them into her lap. Was it possible that Adonijah's feelings coincided with her own? Could he possibly be attracted to her, or was his response merely that of a man's quickly fired desire for a woman? Still, if he could have feelings for her in any way at all, was it possible that her deformity meant nothing to him? Could she really believe him when he said so?

She could see his hand clenching the doorframe, the rigid muscles of his back speaking eloquently of his self-control.

"You truly mean it?" she asked hesitantly.

He glanced over his shoulder, and her heart sank at his controlled expression.

"I mean it. I want you to marry me."

"Then I will do so."

Her hushed voice sounded loudly in the stillness of the room. Adonijah returned to stand before her.

"We will have a traditional wedding," he told her.

Mara's head jerked up in surprise. "No!"

His chin set with determination. "I will not have others think that I am ashamed of you. Nor will I have *you* think so. I will make the arrangements."

Heart sinking, Mara watched him walk quickly through the open door. She began to wonder if she had just made the biggest mistake of her life.

❧

"Are you certain about this, Adonijah?"

Adonijah glanced briefly at Barak's face, which was full of misgivings. His own lips set into a grim line.

"I once asked you about your feelings for Anna," he answered. "You told me to be still. I'm telling you the same now."

A heavy silence hung in the room. Anna rose from the couch and came to stand beside her husband. Placing a hand on his arm, she told him, "Adonijah is old enough to know his own mind." She smiled at Adonijah. "We will do all we can to help. What do you wish of us?"

Although there was a coolness to Barak's demeanor, he seconded his wife's words with a slight nod. Sorry that he had hurt his friend, Adonijah tried to make amends.

"I want Barak to serve as my best man."

Adonijah could see Barak's shoulders relax.

"I will be pleased to do so."

Adonijah grinned ruefully at Anna. "I have no idea what to tell *you*. Only that Mara needs you."

Anna returned his grin wholeheartedly, knowing that it was the idea of a woman's part in the ceremony that he was uneasy about. "Leave it to me," she told him. "When you come for her, she will be ready."

"I have no intention of having a year's betrothal. There is no need. We will be married as soon as it can be arranged."

Barak lifted a brow at this flouting of convention, but then he had nothing to say himself. His own wedding had been as unconventional as a wedding could be.

"Likhi and his wife will be my witnesses. Mara and I will go there this evening. Is it all right if I bring Mara back here afterwards until the wedding can be arranged?"

"Of course," Anna responded quietly. "You know that she is welcome here."

"There is one more thing I would ask of you."

Although Adonijah's eyes were fixed on Barak, his words were meant more for Anna. They waited for him to make his wishes known.

"The harvesting of grapes has begun. Usually, I live in the terrace house to watch over them until harvest is finished, but I would like to purchase the house from you."

Surprised, Barak asked him, "You wish to live there?"

Adonijah nodded.

"But Adonijah," Anna protested. "Both of you are welcome here, you know that."

Barak's gaze met with Adonijah's, and Adonijah knew that his friend understood. The terrace house and property were Anna's dowry left to her by her aunt. All those years ago, Barak had wanted to live there with his wife, but Tirinus's health had declined to the point that Anna felt the need to be close to him. Barak had deferred to her wishes. Still, it had gone against his own desires to do so. To manage another's property was not the same as doing for one's self.

"That, of course, is up to Anna."

Adonijah could see Anna struggling with the things she wanted to say. Her face was filled with doubt. Finally, she told him in a soft voice, "I cannot sell you the property, Adonijah."

Feeling defeated, Adonijah shrugged his shoulders, pressing his lips together. "I understand. The property was a gift from your aunt. I had no right to make such a request."

"You don't understand at all," Anna contradicted. "I can't sell the property to you, because I am *giving* it to you as a gift."

Adonijah opened his mouth to object, but Anna cut him off with a motion of her hand. "Don't argue. After all you have done for Barak and me, I want to do something special for you." She glanced at her husband, and he smiled tenderly back at her.

"I agree."

"Then it's settled," she announced. "Now, I need to see about making arrangements for the wedding."

Bemused at the turn of events, Adonijah left his friends in the triclinium making plans.

≈

"She is my wife and I her husband, from today and forever."

The words that bound Mara and Adonijah left Mara's face white and strained. They were truly betrothed now. The only way to undo it was through a writ of divorce. Although the marriage ceremony wouldn't be for another week, they were considered husband and wife.

A cold lump settled in the pit of Mara's stomach as she thought about the coming ceremony. It was sweet of Adonijah to want to show her that he was not ashamed of her, but the thought of all those people left her terrified. Adonijah had insisted that Mara leave her veil behind. He wanted her to learn to face the world without hiding. Well, if he could stand tall beside a deformed wife, then she could learn to stand tall as well.

Likhi and Martha congratulated them, Likhi's satisfied smile sending Adonijah's eyebrow winging upward in wonder. It was almost as though the old man had planned the whole thing. Shaking his head at such fanciful thoughts, Adonijah took Mara's hand and led her to the cart. He helped her into it, never once raising his eyes to her face for fear that she would see the nervousness that he couldn't seem to control.

Mara waited until Adonijah flicked the whip and they were on their way before she told Adonijah, with some trepidation, "I wish to continue living in my own home until the wedding."

Adonijah glanced at her, shock on his face. "Don't be foolish. I won't allow it."

As her husband, he had the right to command her. How could she make him understand? "Please, Adonijah. It's important to me."

There was no way that he could understand her need to say goodbye to all of her past memories alone. She needed this time to think and strengthen her resolve. And she knew that he would be angry if he found out that she had every intention of fasting for the next three days. Although her body would be weakened even further than it already was, her mind would find strength in communion with Jehovah. She desperately needed that strength.

"Mara."

She met Adonijah's iron determination with a gentle supplication that gave Adonijah pause. Luminous brown eyes brought a quick lump to his throat. She was not demanding, she was pleading, and although it went against everything he believed, he had to agree. Sighing, he told her, "I will come to see you each day and bring you supplies."

Biting her bottom lip to keep from refusing, Mara nodded. It was enough.

❧

Darkness had descended, but the small hut was brightly lit with the lamps of a half dozen young maids, all women who had become friends with Mara through her association with the growing body of believers in Sychar.

Each girl carried a small clay lamp; vials of extra oil swung from cords wrapped around their fingers. The friendly chatter set Mara's already frayed nerves even more on edge.

"You look lovely."

Mara threw Anna a half-smile, knowing that what she said was an impossibility.

"Thank you again, Anna, for all that you have done." Mara glanced down at the lovely white tunic beautifully embellished with embroidery and semiprecious gems. Never in her life had she imagined herself wearing anything so beautiful. When Anna had presented her with the gift, she had almost cried.

She twisted the golden bracelet on her wrist, a wedding gift from Adonijah. Even the golden chains dangling from her ears were from him. She had been overwhelmed at his thoughtfulness, never expecting anything so valuable. He seemed determined to make their wedding as normal as possible.

Anna gave her a quick hug, then reached up and straightened the flower-wreathed crown on Mara's head. She cocked her head to the side, studying Mara from every angle.

"I think you look perfect."

Perfect. Mara thought the word hardly described her, but she was learning that not everyone looked at the outward appearance. The story of Jehovah's choosing of David as a king was one of her favorites. It told how Jehovah looks on the heart, and though Mara knew her heart was also far from perfect, she truly did love the Lord. No, she was not perfect in any way, but she was loved by the One who was.

"The men are coming!"

The excited voice brought Mara out of her reflections, and set her heart to pounding. Glancing out the small window, she could see the lights of dozens of torches moving her way.

Anna placed an arm around her waist, giving her a reassuring hug. Together they watched in silence, broken only by the delighted chatter of the other girls.

When the entourage reached the front door, Adonijah stepped forth and requested to see his bride in a voice that drowned out the chattering voices inside. Acting on her behalf, Anna opened the door to him, while Mara stood behind.

Adonijah opened his mouth to proclaim his treasure, only the words caught in his throat. The soft lamplight reflected off of the jewels in Mara's garment, and she stood before him, a shining presence. In fact, she looked quite beautiful. A slap on his back from Barak brought him to his senses.

"See what a treasure I've found!" he shouted, and the others around him took up the refrain.

"See what a treasure he's found!"

"Look at his treasure!"

Amid the excited chatter and chanting refrains of the others, Barak and Adonijah helped Mara into the litter that would carry her back to Barak's house, where the feasting would be held.

Barak stepped back, and Adonijah moved forward to take Mara's hand. He looked deeply into her eyes. Over the past week, he had been unable to alleviate her fears. "You are beautiful," he told her, and indeed, he said it with such conviction she almost believed him.

Before she could answer, the litter bearers lifted her high and stepped off to the sound of the joyful music. Adonijah released her and took his place beside Barak.

Mara listened to the women's voices lifted in praise of her beauty, and cringed. As with her grandmother's funeral, she felt the hypocrisy of it all. Still, Adonijah had told her that she was beautiful, and honesty had shone from his deep brown eyes. After all, there were more ways to be beautiful than mere appearance. She would do everything in her power to see that he always felt so about her.

When the men began chanting about the groom's bravery and handsomeness, she couldn't help but agree with them. When they spoke of his virility, she colored hotly, thankful that no one could see her face through her wedding veil.

Women and men alike strode along, singing to the music of the lyre, tambourine, and harp. Castanets clacked quickly in time to their tread along the streets. As they moved along in a frenzy of gaiety, the celebrants poured oil, wine, and perfume along the way, while some scattered nuts and grain.

Mara watched amazed. It had never occurred to her that Adonijah had so many friends. Of course, it was considered an insult to refuse an invitation, but these people truly seemed pleased to share in their friend's happiness.

But was he happy? She tried to peer through the crowd

around her to get a better glimpse of Adonijah's face, but it was an impossibility. She settled back against the litter, sighing. For a week now, she had been praying for Jehovah's peace and blessing. She would trust in His answer.

When they arrived at Barak's house, Barak stepped up to his door and pronounced a blessing on the couple, then invited everyone inside.

Adonijah helped Mara from the litter, leading her to a table prepared especially for them. For the next several hours, Mara listened to the toasts and cheers of those around her. Her head began to pound with the tension of the last several hours. She was thankful that Adonijah had chosen to celebrate only one night instead of the traditional seven.

Adonijah got to his feet to propose a toast to his bride. When his eyes met hers, Mara's widened in surprise at the emotion she saw lurking in their depths. For only a moment did she see the intensity of his expression before it disappeared so quickly she thought that she might have imagined it. Her mouth went suddenly very dry.

"To my wife," Adonijah told the room at large, but his sparkling eyes were on Mara. For the first time since Adonijah had offered for her in marriage, Mara began to worry about the coming night.

nine

The evening progressed with agonizing slowness, to Adonijah's way of thinking. He watched Mara as her shoulders drooped wearily, obviously as exhausted as he was. The past week had been busy, but also full of tension. Pushing his own shoulders back, he revolved them slowly to try and work out some of the kinks.

For a moment, his mind went back to when Anna had opened the door for him to claim his bride. He had been stunned by the picture Mara had made standing in the glow from the bridesmaids' oil lamps. She had seemed almost to shimmer with an unearthly light. The reflection of the jewels on her bridal dress had intensified the luminosity of her amber brown eyes that peeked out from behind her veil, and her whole being seemed lit from within by a special glow. If not for Barak's hearty slap on his back, he would probably still be standing there gawking at her.

They had repeated their vows to Jehovah before the assembled guests. Since Mara's grandmother was not alive, Anna had taken it upon herself to act in Bilhah's stead. She made a mixture of henna leaves, then the guests took turns dipping their hands in the mixture and rubbing it on his and Mara's clasped hands.

Adonijah absently massaged the orange coloring on his skin, his eyes straying once again to his wife. Even the word sent prickles of ice skittering through his midsection. What had seemed a logical act before suddenly took on a deeper meaning.

He tried to keep his mind from returning to the kiss that

they had shared, but his unruly thoughts persisted. How had a kiss meant to convey friendship gotten so out of hand? Even now, thinking about it made the blood flow like molten lava through his body.

His eyes met Mara's, and he read the fearful uncertainty there. Had his inner musings been apparent to even one so inexperienced? Using his iron will, he forcefully brought his thoughts into subjection. As the fire left his eyes, Mara hesitantly returned his feigned smile.

His attention was diverted when several people rose to leave. Before long, others joined them until only a handful remained.

Adonijah squeezed Mara's shoulder lightly. "You must be tired."

Her pale features were answer enough. She opened her mouth to object, but Adonijah didn't allow her the chance to speak.

"Let us retire for the night. We have a long day before us on the morrow."

Mara placed her hand in his, her mind suddenly gone blank. What did Adonijah expect of her now? They really hadn't had much time to discuss their marriage, and now the apprehension left her with a sudden desire to fling Adonijah's hand from her and run screaming from the house. She quickly quelled the impulse.

Adonijah pulled her to her feet, his reassuring smile a sudden balm to her chaotic thoughts. Whatever happened, he was still her friend. His eyes were reiterating that fact once again.

Taking a deep breath, she followed him from the room and along the passage to the bedroom that Adonijah had always occupied alone. Her smile wavered, and then disappeared altogether. Adonijah was quick to notice.

"You needn't be afraid," he told her softly. "Although we

will share a bed, we will share nothing else until we're both ready. Understand?"

Mara wasn't so certain that she did. For some reason she had assumed that she and Adonijah would sleep apart. Adonijah interrupted her thoughts.

"I have a few things to attend to before coming to bed. I'll see you later."

He bent and kissed her cheek lightly, then disappeared down the corridor. Mara watched him go, her ego sinking lower than the sunset. What things did he have to do this late at night? Was he just making it up so that he wouldn't have to be with her? Still, the idea had obviously been his to share a bed. Pushing her palms against her temples, Mara tried to slow her mind from its rushing pace. Adonijah was right. Not only was she tired, she was exhausted, and her imagination was running away with her.

Although she had ended her fast three days earlier, her body hadn't had time to recover from its ordeal. The queasy turn of her stomach told her she still had a long way to go. Adonijah had done as he said he would and brought her provisions, but until three days ago they had remained untouched. Now, she was definitely feeling the effects. Her body was shaking—whether from that, or from fear, she still wasn't certain.

Did she trust Adonijah? She had at first believed so, but now the realization had come to her that she had committed herself to a man until death, and that said man now had complete authority over her.

She carefully removed her wedding dress and laid it gently over the chest resting at the foot of the bed. Her fingers trailed over the garment as she moved to replace it with the one prepared for her wedding night. Another gift from Anna.

Mara pulled the soft, silky white tunic over her body and felt herself relax. There was something to be said for pure silk. Something about the texture was soothing as it glided smoothly over the skin—massaging, relaxing. Anna's intention, no doubt.

When she climbed beneath the covers of the bed, she realized that Anna must have been at work here also. The silk sheets embraced her warmly, and Mara snuggled deep into their folds. Stretching like a sleek Egyptian cat, she almost purred with contentment.

Pushing thoughts of Adonijah from her mind, Mara began her nightly conversation with her Lord. He had come to be the one surety in her otherwise turbulent universe.

Are you there, Lord?

A peaceful feeling surrounded her, much like the warmth from the silk sheets. Yes, her Lord was with her. He had promised never to forsake her, and He would keep that promise. Whatever happened, she could count on that.

Her drowsy eyes fluttered closed and she sank into peaceful oblivion.

❧

Adonijah looked down on his sleeping wife and smiled. She was curled up like a little child, her hands folded beneath her marked cheek. He watched her for some time, listening to her breath coming in soft little bursts. He suddenly found his own breathing reacting in an odd way.

Frowning, he moved away from her to stare out the window. Often he had stood thus, thinking of Mara and what he could do to help her. Somewhere along the way his feelings of friendship, guilt, and obligation had become intertwined until he wasn't certain *what* he felt anymore. He knew he liked Mara, but how far did that like go?

His thoughts kept returning to that one fiery kiss they had shared. Mara's response had certainly surprised him, but no more than his own. He had been able to think of little else since that time.

Glancing back at the bed, he wondered how on earth he was

supposed to sleep beside her if he couldn't clear his mind of such thoughts. He had promised her safety, and he wouldn't go back on his word. But would he be able to keep it?

After readying himself for bed, he dropped to his knees and began to petition the Lord. Only with Jehovah's strength could he hope to keep to the course he had decided for himself. Only with Jehovah's strength could he hope to quiet the wild feelings that seemed to be tearing him apart.

He climbed into the bed, pushing the silken sheets from him. The wine they had drunk in celebration had left him feeling too warm, and his head was slightly fuzzy. Since Barak had brought out his finest vintage instead of the milder, less flavorful wine that they normally drank with their meals, it had a more intoxicating effect on the body.

In her sleep, Mara curled against his side, and he felt again that jolt as though he had been struck by lightning. Her breath brushed his shoulder, making his skin tingle, but instead of increasing his desire, oddly, it had the opposite effect.

Her childlike innocence touched a protective chord deep inside his heart. Brushing the hair from her face, he kissed her softly on her forehead, pulling her snugly into his arms. The words that the Apostle Paul had spoken thrummed in time to his accelerated heartbeat. *Love is patient. Love is patient. Love is patient.*

He smiled wryly. Patience was not one of his greater virtues, but then again, neither was he in love. Still, for the first time, he admitted to himself that he wanted Mara. He wanted Mara the way a man wants a woman he is attracted to, yet there was a subtle difference to his desire from the times he had experienced it in the past. He couldn't quite put his finger on it, but there *was* a difference.

Years ago in his home of Jotapata, Miriam had teased him with her flashing eyes and coy smiles, and he had felt a similar burning desire for her. It shamed him all over again just thinking of it now, for she had belonged to Barak. Or so he had thought. When he found out that Barak had no desire to marry Miriam, he had been elated, hoping that there might be a chance for him. But Jehovah had other plans, and now here he was married to a woman he really barely knew. One that others thought of as being cursed and ugly.

What was there about Mara that caused him to overlook her deformity and suddenly yearn for her kisses? When he looked at her, his heart hammered within him and reason left him. Was he perhaps in love after all? Or was this just another example of a reckless infatuation? How could he know for certain whether his heart was as involved as his body?

Until he did, he must keep his thoughts and feelings to himself, because he had made a promise to Mara, and he would keep that promise if it killed him.

He began to pray for guidance, as well as strength.

ঌ

Mara smiled as Anna waved at yet another worker in the vineyards. As far as Mara knew, there wasn't anyone who didn't love her gentle friend.

Anna shifted her position on the wagon seat and turned to Mara.

"Not far now," she told Mara. "The terrace house is just around that bend in the road."

Mara glanced behind her to the contents of the wagon. Barak and Anna had given Adonijah and herself the pieces of furniture and other household goods. Mara had been overwhelmed by their generosity.

"Anna," she began hesitantly. "You have done so much for Adonijah and myself. I can never thank you enough."

Anna's smile reached all the way to her hazel eyes. She squeezed Mara's hand gently.

"It was nothing." Her face became suddenly serious. "How can I begin to explain to you how much your friendship has meant to me? For years, I was an only child. Then there was Barak." Her nose wrinkled charmingly. "But he is a man, and though I love him dearly, he cannot understand the things of a woman."

She checked the team of horses as they drifted to the left of the road, bringing them back to the center. Although she kept her gaze on the road, her words continued.

"My babies and my family keep me from being lonely, but it has been so nice to have another woman to talk to."

"But Anna," Mara protested. "You have so *many* friends."

Anna nodded. "True, but I have never been close to another woman until I met you. I don't understand it, but I feel like I have known you all my life. You have become the sister I never had."

In silence, Mara considered her friend's words. Everything Anna said was equally true for her as well. The bond of friendship that had sprung up between the two was unexplainable, but also undeniable. Anna's next words interrupted her thoughts.

"There's the house."

After years of living in mud huts, this building was a joy to behold. Although it couldn't compare with the villa that Anna called home, it was, nonetheless, an extraordinary building. Mara caught her breath at the grandeur of it all.

Since this house was considered only a temporary living quarters for the family during the harvesting of grapes, Mara had expected something far less elaborate. In most cases, families had just a temporary mud hut to live in until the season of grapes was over. This one was made of the finest dressed stone, exquisitely inlaid with fine cedar. As her wide-eyed look wandered over the structure, it suddenly occurred to her just how wealthy Tirinus must be.

Adonijah came out of the door that led to the center courtyard. He paused a moment, watching as Anna drew the wagon to a halt beside the hitching post. Quickly, he took the reins from her and wrapped them around the pole. Smiling, he helped Anna from the wagon and then came to Mara. Lifting her to the ground, his questioning eyes met hers.

"Do you like it?"

Mara made a small sound. "Like it? How could anyone help but like it? It's beautiful! I never expected. . ."

Her voice trailed off at the look on his face. Swallowing hard, she pushed out of his hold and turned to Anna. "Why didn't you tell me?"

Anna shrugged. "Truthfully, I never even thought about it; but even if I had, it was Adonijah's surprise, and therefore his to tell."

Adonijah took Mara's arm and began leading her towards the house. "Anna has had servants cleaning the house for days, although I have never known it to be anything other than in good order. Barak is on the roof making a few repairs," he told Anna. "I was helping him until I saw the wagon approach."

Mara hurried ahead of him, anxious to see the rest of the house. The central courtyard contained several doors leading to other rooms, and the leather soles of her sandals tapped across the paved flagstones as she went to investigate. Judging from the number of doors, there had to be at least six other enclosures.

The first door she came to led into a room that would be considered the main reception hall. The red, black, yellow, and white mosaic tiles that formed an elaborate design in the floor sparkled after their fresh cleaning. Inlaid shelves lined the walls, their niches just waiting for items to be added as decoration. Already, Mara could picture her pots resting there.

Another door opened into a bathroom also elaborately tiled with mosaic stones. The step-down bath was already filled with water, its cool surface inviting in the late afternoon heat.

What thrilled Mara the most was the separate kitchen area. Here there were inlaid niches in the walls to hold her cookware, but a separate door led outside to the cook oven. There was also a small oven inside for cold and wet weather.

Not realizing she did so, Mara sighed with happiness.

"You like it?" Adonijah asked again.

Mara's eyes shone like gemstones, but she was bereft of words. What could she possibly say? She settled for a vehement nod of the head.

"There are three bedrooms," Anna told her, interrupting Adonijah's eye contact. "When the time comes, we can add more."

Mara's face flooded with color. She couldn't for the life of her meet Adonijah's look, nor Anna's. Instead, she turned back to the open doorway.

"I suppose we should start to unload the wagon."

The afternoon sun was waning when they finished unloading. Anna had left the arranging of contents for Mara, knowing how important it was for a woman to make a house her own. Mara was grateful. Still, she nervously watched Anna and Barak climb into the wagon for the return trip. In just a moment, she and Adonijah would be alone. Part of her longed for this to be so, but another part was terrified. What would they find to talk about? To do?

When she had awakened this morning, Adonijah had already left the villa. He had told her the night before that there were a few repairs left to make to the house. She wondered if he was sensitive to her feelings, realizing that come morning she would be filled with embarrassment. Only with Anna by her side had she been able to face him with equanimity.

Now, they would be totally alone. The terrace house was several miles from Anna's villa, and at first she had been delighted with the thought of being on her own again. Now, watching the wagon disappear around the curve, she felt uncommonly empty. She reflected that if theirs had been a true marriage, this would probably not have been so.

Her eyes met Adonijah's briefly. He was watching her, his dark eyes enigmatic.

"There are things I need to see to," he told her.

"As do I. I must see to preparing our supper."

Adonijah shook his head, smiling slightly at the color blooming in her cheeks. "Not tonight. Anna sent us enough food to last for several days. I put it in the kitchen."

They stood staring at each other, neither knowing what else to say. Mara felt more uncomfortable than she could ever remember feeling. Adonijah leaned forward and kissed her on her mouth, then grinning, he turned and left her staring after him.

Flustered, Mara clenched her hands at her side. What was he trying to say with these actions? Gentle, loving, kind, he left her defenseless against the feelings she was trying so hard to hide. He wasn't making it very easy on her.

What would Adonijah do if she turned on him, throwing her arms around his neck and inviting further kisses? For just a moment she became a true daughter of Eve, her mouth curling upwards as she dreamed about what might happen.

Shaking herself from such thoughts, she chastised herself severely. If she wanted this marriage with Adonijah to work, she would have to accept his overtures of friendship as just what they were intended. She needed to stop seeing every little kindness as a desire on his part to win her favor. After all, he showed the same favor to his nephew and niece.

Going back into the house, she began to put things where she wanted them to go. The first necessity was to arrange the lamps where they could be lit against the fast approaching darkness.

When she finished this task her hands were shaking, and she realized just how tired she was. Her body began to tremble at the unaccustomed work of the past several hours. Quickly, she found the food supplies in the kitchen and fixed herself something to eat.

There was a small stone vat in the corner, where water pumped from a nearby spring flowed from lead pipes. Here Adonijah had placed a container of goat milk, the water continually sliding over it as it rested in the vat. Lifting the flask, she poured herself a cup of the milk, marveling at the coolness of it as it slid down her parched throat.

This house boasted amenities she had never encountered in her life. For a moment, she felt guilty as she thought about those from the poor community who had to eke out a living by surviving off of the charity of others, or else by backbreaking work. Again, she wondered at Jehovah's blessing her life so. Closing her eyes, she gave sincere thanks to the Creator of it all.

&

Adonijah leaned against the parapet surrounding the packed clay roof. Blowing out through his lips, he lifted his face to the starlit sky. There was but one thought in his mind. To woo, and win, his wife.

He grinned slightly as he remembered her startled reaction to his kiss. That she was surprised was obvious. That she hadn't turned from him was a miracle. He knew, without conceit, that his wife was stirred by his kisses. Given time, he also knew that they could have a normal marriage and be happy here in this lovely house.

There was but one flaw in this plan. Mara still thought herself unlovable. Having accepted Christ as her Savior, she still found it hard to believe that others could love her as Jehovah loved her.

Frowning, he turned and leaned his back against the parapet. Although he desired his wife, he was still having a hard time deciding whether he *loved* her. The Greeks had several words for love. *Agapé* was a perfect love, the kind where a person could love others even when they were his enemies. This was the hardest kind of all to maintain, but it was the one that all Christians were commanded to have for one another. It wasn't a feeling; it was a decision. A commanding of the will.

Then there was *eros* love. He smiled wryly. That love he understood all too well. It was a love that was physical, and where agapé love was eternal, eros could flash into fire and burn itself out in an instant.

Phileo love was what a friend felt for another friend. It was a feeling of goodwill, but not very intense.

Then there was *storgé* love, the kind that families experience. He felt such love for Barak, Anna, Ramoth, and Samah.

Which led him back to his original thought. *Was he in love with his wife?* Did any of these Greek words suffice to express his feelings where Mara was concerned? Yes, he realized, they *all* did. Unfortunately, now that he had discovered that, he was more confused than ever. Until he had things straight in his mind, he needed to keep his distance, and give Mara time to discover her own feelings. There was only one problem with such a thought. He was not a patient man.

ten

Mara's life fell into a familiar routine, and if she was not completely happy, she was, for the most part, content. The only thing that marred her happiness was the wall that Adonijah seemed to have erected between them. Although he was considerate, and kind to a fault, he held himself in reserve, as though he wanted to keep her at a distance.

To an extent, she could understand how he must be feeling. He was trying so hard to show her that he cared for her as a friend, but it must be trying for him to have to walk such a fine line for fear that she would take his intentions seriously.

To that end she tried to make it easier on him by being cool and polite, but refraining from anything he might construe as affection on her part. Instead of appreciating it, he seemed to grow more irritated with each passing day. Mara was beginning to wonder if he was already regretting his decision to marry her. She had considered talking with Anna about it, but she decided against it. It seemed somehow disrespectful to discuss her husband behind his back. King Solomon spoke of a virtuous wife being one that a husband would have full confidence in. She wanted to be like that woman, and someday maybe Adonijah would rise up and call her blessed. Grinning at the thought, she began kneading yesterday's leaven into today's flour.

Each day Adonijah went to the vineyards to oversee the workers and Mara stayed behind, content to do the things of a normal housewife.

The first thing every morning she baked their bread for the day. After adding the small clump of dough from the previous day's bread for leavening, she would knead the flour into a dough ready to be rolled into flat cakes and baked. Since this required more time than thought, she often found her mind flitting from one subject to another. At first, she had thought this might be a good time to pray, but she soon found it impossible to rein in her thoughts enough to concentrate.

Since they had moved into this house, Adonijah had taken to coming to bed later and later. She missed the shared companionship of their earlier relationship and wondered what had happened to cause Adonijah to change so. He often seemed tense, preoccupied. It began to put her on edge whenever he was around. Not knowing how to put things back on their original footing, she left it in Jehovah's hands. Whatever was upsetting Adonijah, she certainly hoped it was resolved quickly.

Adding a little honey to the dough for flavoring, she then prepared to take her bread to the outside oven for baking. The hot days of summer made it far too warm to bake inside.

It took longer to bake the bread than usual since she was baking twice the amount. The Sabbath would begin at sunset, and she needed to have everything in readiness for their meals tomorrow.

Placing a small pot over the hole in the top of the cone-shaped oven, Mara added water and lentils for their supper tonight. She mixed in some onions, garlic, and salt, wishing that she had some other vegetables to add. The supplies Anna had given them were long since gone, and since Mara had not lived here long enough to get a garden going, she was finding it difficult to supplement their meals the way she would have liked. Still, it was far better than living off of only bread.

After the first rains, she would prepare the ground behind the house for her own garden. Ever since she was a child, she had loved the feeling of the earth running through her fingers and watching things grow. In this way, she and Adonijah were much alike. Even now, she had managed to coax several herbs to grow in small pots that she had accumulated in her kitchen. Not only were they useful, they added a bright spot of color to the room.

Adonijah thought it strange that she had plants in pots scattered all around their house, and not all of them were functional. To Mara it didn't matter if they served a purpose or not, she just loved the feeling of outdoors that they brought to a home.

The sun was reaching its zenith when she finally finished everything she wanted to cook for the next two days.

Trying to find some relief from the oppressive heat, she took her laundry to the roof. Although the courtyard was large enough for washing clothes, the roof was much cooler.

She had just finished with the last robe when a shout from below brought her to the edge of the roof. Leaning over the parapet, she noticed a Roman soldier waiting in front of their house for an answer to his summons. He tied his horse to the post in front of their door, all the while searching the area with his eyes.

Mara bit her lip in indecision. Should she go down and see what he wanted, or should she pretend not to be at home? The one she was reluctant to do; the other she knew was dishonest. Taking her courage in hand, she called to the soldier from her vantage point on the roof.

"Yes?"

He took a step backwards, craning his neck to see her.

"I would like some water for my horse."

Mara looked past him to the well just beyond the trees. "There's a well over there," she told him, pointing. "Help yourself."

His oblique glance settled on her for just a moment before he untied the horse and moved to the shaded coolness beneath the trees. He removed his helmet, running his hands through hair darkened by perspiration. Although she was quite a distance from him, Mara could tell that he was very young.

All the things Grandmother had taught her about hospitality rose up to shame her. Although Jews were known for their hospitality among their own kind, it had always been forbidden to associate with Gentiles. Now she knew that Jehovah saw no difference between the two. The Apostle Paul had reminded the believers that some, in their hospitality, had entertained angels unaware. This man in all his Roman regalia certainly didn't look like any angel she had imagined.

Forcing herself down the stairs, she went to the kitchen and poured a cup of water from the cool spring water that ran through their kitchen.

Seated on a large boulder, the soldier raised his head when he saw her coming across the ground towards her. When she stood before him, his face lifted to hers, his surprise evident.

Mara handed him the cup of water, carefully avoiding personal contact.

"Although the cistern water is fine for horses, this water is much better for people."

Slowly, he reached out his hand to take the cup, his eyes studying her suspiciously. He glanced at the water as though it might contain some kind of poison.

"May I get you something to eat? Some bread perhaps?"

He jerked his look back to her, his mouth slightly parting. "I am hungry," he agreed hesitantly.

Mara smiled and the soldier dubiously returned it.

"Wait here and I will bring you something."

She could feel his eyes following her as she returned to the house. Slipping inside, she leaned back against the closed door, one hand clutching her chest. The drumming of her heart was beginning to slow its erratic pace as her fear receded.

Taking a plate, she placed on it a loaf of the honey bread and some fresh grapes. When she gave them to the soldier, he smiled his appreciation.

"I have work to do," Mara told him. "If you don't mind, I will return to my chores. Is there anything else that I can get you?"

He slowly shook his head, his eyes intent as they studied her face. Mara's hands itched to reach up and cover the mark, but she refrained. The soldier didn't seem repelled by what he saw; for that she was thankful.

Mara started to turn away, but the soldier called to her. Unwillingly, she gave him her attention.

"You are a Jew?" he wanted to know.

For a moment she wasn't certain how to answer. Finally, she told him in a voice firm with conviction, "I am a Christian."

His eyes narrowed to slits, but his face remained inscrutable. Mara couldn't tell what he was thinking.

"I've met others like you," he said, as though speaking to himself. "I repeat, are you a Jew or are you a Gentile?"

"I am a Jewish Christian."

He rose to stand before her, and Mara took a hasty step backwards. The Roman towered over her, making her feel small in comparison. Although he was younger than Adonijah, the two would compare in height and build, and whereas her husband had grown back his beard, the soldier was clean shaven. His eyes were as blue as the sky, and they studied her thoroughly. He handed her the cup and plate, brushing the dust from his garments as he did so. His handsome face creased into a genuine smile.

Taking the utensils, Mara dropped her gaze to her feet as he continued to stare at her.

"I thought all Jews hated all Romans."

The huskiness of his voice sent Mara's eyes flying upwards to meet his. His expression was carefully blank, but she sensed a strange undercurrent of tension.

"Christians try to love everyone," she answered uncertainly.

"Love?" His lips twisted with mockery. "I somehow doubt we have the same thoughts when speaking that word."

Mara's face colored crimson at his look. Clutching the cup and plate to her breast, she couldn't again look him in the eye.

"Thank you for the refreshments," he said, pulling his horse forward. He paused a moment as though he wanted to say more. With her eyes cast to the ground, she couldn't see him, but she heard when he mounted his horse.

"For your information," he told her, and Mara was finally able to bring herself to look at him, "my name is Trajan. And your name is?"

Reluctantly, she answered him.

His look was intense, and Mara suddenly found herself wanting to flee.

"Well, Mara," he told her softly. "I will remember your kindness."

Just exactly what he meant by that, she had no idea. His eyes once again scanned her from head to foot, and nodding, he took his leave. She watched him until he was out of sight, pondering his words. Shrugging her shoulders, she returned to the house.

&

"You there!"

Adonijah glanced up from his work to see a Roman soldier standing on the road below him. The boy standing beside Adonijah made a slight sound, and Adonijah hushed him to silence.

Lifting a dark eyebrow, Adonijah asked, "Are you speaking to me?"

"Either one of you," the soldier snapped in irritation.

It was then that Adonijah noticed all the equipment at the man's feet. Lifting his eyes to meet the soldier's, he knew what was coming before the soldier even opened his mouth.

"I need one of you to help me carry this equipment."

Hearing the arrogance in the Roman's voice, Adonijah could feel the young boy at his side tense. He handed the boy his pruning hook.

"Stay here, Ithacar. I'll go."

"But—"

Adonijah quieted him with a look. "Continue with your work. I'll return as soon as possible."

Making his way down the hill, Adonijah took the opportunity to send up a petition to Jehovah to help him keep his temper. Roman law required that those asked by soldiers to carry their gear must do so for a mile. It rankled him that he would have to leave his own work to do so.

When he reached the soldier's side, his look moved over the equipment. There really was far too much for one man to carry, and especially in this heat. His questioning gaze met the soldier's irate one.

"My horse bolted as I was coming down the hill," he told Adonijah peevishly. "He stepped in a hole and broke his leg. I had to put him down."

Without answering, Adonijah reached down and lifted some of the bags at the Roman's feet.

"Which way?"

The soldier motioned towards the south. "I'm heading for the garrison in Jerusalem."

Turning, Adonijah began to lead the way. They walked in silence for some time before the soldier finally asked, "Have you been to Jerusalem?"

Adonijah nodded. "A few times."

They walked again in silence, Adonijah fighting old prejudices. Although he had managed to overcome his aversion to Samaritans, that grace had never been extended to the Romans. Anger churned inside him when he thought of his homeland invaded by these people. Had he argued with the man about carrying his gear, he very well could have found himself in prison, if not hanging on a cross.

That thought brought Jesus so vividly to mind, it was as though he could see Him physically hanging on the cross at Golgotha. Having never set eyes on his Savior before, it amazed him that the image seemed so clear.

Words that the Apostle Peter had shared with them came to his mind. Jesus had said that if any man forced you to go with him a mile, go with him two. Still, *legally* he only needed to go *one* mile.

When they reached the first mile marker the soldier stopped. Dropping his portion of the gear at his feet, he began searching the area to see if there was another he could press into service. The fields around them were empty of all human occupation. Sighing, he turned back to Adonijah.

"I'll take that now," he told him, indicating the bags Adonijah was carrying.

Unwillingly, Adonijah was impressed by the man's honesty. It wasn't unusual for a Roman to coerce someone into carrying his gear farther than the lawful mile. Most people were too afraid to object, which didn't make the Romans very popular in these parts.

"I will carry it for another mile."

The soldier's mouth dropped open in surprise, but he was no more surprised than Adonijah himself. Adonijah couldn't believe that he had actually made the offer.

Turning, Adonijah continued on his way, and the soldier scrambled to pick up his tackle and follow after him. Adonijah could feel the man's look, although he refused to acknowledge it. He kept up a steady pace, already peeved with himself for agreeing to assist the man.

"Well, that makes two surprises in one day," the soldier joked.

Adonijah glanced his way briefly, but said nothing.

"Before I reached your fields," the Roman continued, "I stopped at a house on the hill."

Adonijah tensed, his gaze jerking back to the soldier. His attention diverted, he tripped on a rock, but then quickly righted himself.

"There was a Jewish woman there, and although I only asked for a drink for my horse, she gave *me* one as well." He turned to Adonijah. "You're a Jew, aren't you?"

Since Adonijah was wearing his Hebrew overcoat, his heritage was obvious. He turned away from the soldier's regard, afraid that the Roman would see the hostility burning in his eyes. "I am."

The soldier continued talking as though to himself. "She had a strange birthmark on her face, but her eyes were lovely—dark and peaceful. A man could lose his way in such eyes." He stopped speaking, his eyes staring off into the distance. He continued slowly, "I have always thought that the eyes were a window to a person's soul. If so, then this woman was quite beautiful."

The anger grew within Adonijah. This soldier was speaking of his wife, and there was something in his voice that set Adonijah's teeth on edge.

"She said she was a Jewish Christian," he told Adonijah. "I've met Christians before. There's something different about them. When Mara spoke of love, she really meant it." He shook his head, perplexed. "I don't understand. How can someone love his enemies?"

"She spoke of love?" Adonijah asked him through gritted teeth. He couldn't have been more surprised if the soldier had told him that the Jews had suddenly conquered Rome. How dare the man call his wife by her given name!

Unaware of Adonijah's rising ire, the soldier nodded. Taking a cloth from his bag, he wiped the perspiration from his brow. "She said Christians try to love everyone."

The words pierced Adonijah, and he felt some of his anger ebb. Although he had been a Christian much longer than Mara, Mara was practicing what she had been taught. It was that very gentleness that had reached out to this young soldier and had him wondering about Christianity.

The fact that he, Adonijah, was burning with jealousy was beside the point. He knew there would be no jealousy if there was trust, but his and Mara's relationship hadn't grown to that point. Now, this young, handsome Roman spoke of his wife with something akin to reverence and he felt his insides churn with resentment.

"Do you know about Christians?"

The soldier's question brought Adonijah's thinking back to the present. That the man even had to ask told Adonijah more than he cared to know. His own attitude had been less than Christlike. Although he had offered to carry the man's gear an extra mile, his heart hadn't been in it. Suddenly, he was ashamed of his thoughts and feelings.

"Yes, I know about Christians," he answered softly. "I am one."

For a moment, the soldier just stared at him. When their eyes met, it was as though the Roman could see inside Adonijah's mind. For the first time, he seemed to recognize the anger seething there, and somehow sensed its cause. "Oh," he finally said, and spoke no more.

They continued on their way, both quiet with their own thoughts. When they reached the next mile marker, the Roman spotted another man in the field to their left. Calling him over, he had Adonijah give the man his gear.

Adonijah could sense the Samaritan's burning resentment against the disdainful Roman. Hadn't he felt much the same way himself? Stifling the impulse to offer to carry the Roman's bags yet another mile, Adonijah watched them go. Turning, he began to hurry back the way he had just traversed.

The sun was waning in the sky, its fiery rays changing the featherlight clouds to hues of purple and red. He needed to be home before the Sabbath began, and that was just a few short hours away. Judging the time and distance, he began to run.

eleven

Adonijah never mentioned the Roman on the road, and neither did Mara. The fact that she didn't had Adonijah suddenly smoldering with suspicions.

He should have known that if *he* could see past her deformity to the beauty within, others would also be able to do so. His mind was filled with doubts about whether he had done right by marrying Mara, knowing that she didn't love him. It occurred to him that if he had waited, perhaps she would have found the love she was looking for.

Her unhappy demeanor of late only increased his misgivings. In consequence, he became even more distant than before.

Now, here he was pacing the roof of their home while Mara slept peacefully within. He had told her that he wanted to spend time in the cooler temperatures of the roof, but he was fairly certain that she knew that wasn't altogether true.

Tomorrow, they would leave for Jerusalem to celebrate the Feast of Booths. Both Anna and Mara were excited. He, however, was more than a little fearful. Jews from every area of Palestine would travel to Jerusalem to celebrate the ending of the grape harvest and pay honor to the day set aside by Jehovah in remembrance of their wilderness wandering. Jerusalem would be a seething mass of humanity, and among them, the usual zealots and cutthroats. A menacing darkness seemed to settle around him. Shrugging off the feeling, he turned his mind to other thoughts.

Mara had diffidently suggested that she wear her veils, but he had firmly denounced such a notion. When Mara had adamantly refused to go otherwise, he had finally relented. He still couldn't understand why she was so reticent about her deformity, but then neither had he had to suffer the injustices that both she and Bilhah had experienced in their lives.

Taking a deep breath of the cool night air, he was finally able to settle his churning thoughts, and lying down on the woven mat he had brought up to the roof, he studied the glowing stars above him. Sighing, he closed his eyes and allowed the cool breeze to waft gently over him, soothing him into a restful slumber.

❧

The road to Jerusalem was filled with weary, yet excited, pilgrims once again making the trek to the most holy city of the Jews. Only in Samaria were the roadways free of travelers, for Samaritans denounced Jerusalem as God's holy city; they did their worshiping on Mount Gerazim. Since Samaria was anathema to most Jews, the crowd hadn't intensified until they reached the joining roads farther south.

For Mara it was both a thrilling, and a frightening, experience. In all of her wanderings with her grandmother, they had never gone to Jerusalem. Perhaps Bilhah thought that devout Jews would have turned on Mara for desecrating their holy city with her marked presence. Even now, the thought gave her pause.

Mara's gaze went to her husband striding along before her, Barak keeping pace at his side. She was calmed by the realization that her husband was there to take care of her, and though she would do all that she could to avoid any confrontations, she was still afraid that something might happen.

Anna interrupted her thoughts.

"My Aunt Bithnia will be delighted to welcome you," she tried to reassure Mara.

Mara realized that her fears must have been reflected on her face. She gave Anna a half smile. "I hope so."

"You will see," Anna replied confidently. "And Barak's mother will be thrilled to see *all* of us. It's been a long time since we have been to Jerusalem."

"I have never been to Jerusalem," Mara returned quietly.

"Never?"

Mara shook her head, but refrained from explanation. Anna would no doubt draw her own conclusions, and they most probably would be correct ones. To break the awkward silence that had settled between them, Anna began to describe the city of Jerusalem. She shifted Samah from one hip to the other.

"Here. Let me," Mara begged, reaching for the child. Samah's little arms readily reached for Mara, her small features wreathed with delight.

Anna smiled. "She certainly does love you."

Mara glanced up from tickling Samah beneath her chin. Her eyes searched Anna's face for any sign of displeasure, but there was none. The same loving smile Anna gave her daughter, she bestowed on Mara as well. Relieved, Mara smiled back, though Anna couldn't see her through the veils she used to hide her birthmark.

"The feeling is mutual."

The sky was a hazy blue, the sun warm as they trekked along the dusty road. Before long, Adonijah dropped back to walk beside them. His glance raked his wife from head to foot, and he frowned.

"Surely it's not necessary to wear your veils yet," he admonished, his voice laced with irritation.

Mara glanced around the small caravan of people they were a part of. Though most of them were friends, many were not. Several strangers had joined their group along the way, since traveling in company was preferred to traveling alone.

"I think it is."

She could sense his disapproval, though he made no further comment.

"Barak and I need to gather as many myrtle, palm, olive, and other branches as we can. The closer we get to Jerusalem, the shorter the supply will be."

"Enough for two booths?" Anna asked him.

"At least," he agreed. "We have no idea what Tirinus or Bithnia has planned, but Barak is fairly certain that Tamar will want to spend the time with him."

At mention of Barak's mother, Mara's heart froze. Since Barak's father had adopted Adonijah so long ago, Tamar was considered Adonijah's mother, as well as Barak's. She felt more than a little apprehensive of the reception she would receive from her mother-in-law. Tamar hadn't been able to make it to their wedding, so Mara had yet to meet her. What would she think of having a deformed daughter-in-law?

Adonijah rejoined Barak, and the two men periodically left the road to gather branches from nearby trees. They placed them on the cart with Ramoth, who for once was behaving himself.

Mara smiled at the boy as he bobbed along in the donkey-drawn cart. "Do you know the meaning behind these branches?"

Ramoth nodded solemnly. "My father explained it to me. When we get to Jerusalem, we will build booths to live in for seven days, just like the Israelites did in the desert."

Although his voice was serious, there was an excited sparkle in his wide brown eyes. Mara smiled behind her veils.

"We get to sleep outside in booths," he told her, and Mara felt certain that this was the sole reason he was so delighted.

Anna smiled slightly. "Remember what you promised, Ramoth."

He nodded, his look once again fixing on Mara. "I promised

to be good. Father says that if I cause any trouble, I will never be allowed to go to Jerusalem again."

Mara was thankful that Ramoth couldn't see behind her veils because she couldn't help but grin. It remained to be seen whether the boy could keep his promise.

Anna once again began to tell stories about Jerusalem. Since Ramoth had been but a babe the last time they had gone, he was as fascinated by Anna's descriptions as Mara was.

Anna sighed. "The holy City of David, and yet so many reject the Messiah. Every day, persecution by the Jews grows. Even those Jews who accept the Christ refuse to accept His Gentile children."

Mara well understood rejection. "What do they do?"

"The Christian Jews refuse to eat or socialize with the Gentile believers. The Apostle Paul even had to rebuke the Apostle Peter for doing the same. He had to remind him that Jesus gave salvation to the Gentiles as well. The Lord went so far as to send Peter a vision to verify it. Still, the Jews choose to remain set apart. With one side of their mouth they thank Jehovah for saving the Gentiles, with the other they deny them the right of kinship."

"You're not a Jew," Mara reminded her. "Why then do you go to Jerusalem for the Feast of Booths?"

Anna smiled. "I go with my husband. The Jews still believe in keeping the ordinances of the old law. They still believe it's what sets them apart as God's people."

"Perhaps it's following the old traditions that keeps the Jews from accepting the Gentiles."

The smile left Anna's face. "Old traditions die hard. Paul said that there was one body and one Spirit, yet in Jerusalem there are separate assemblies for the Christian Gentiles and for the Christian Jews. I am afraid that before long there won't be *one* church, because so many things are causing divisiveness among the believers."

Mara remembered the conversation she had had with Adonijah. "Like circumcision, you mean?"

Anna nodded. "That's one thing. The argument has grown hotter over the need for Gentiles to be circumcised. Many Jews, though they call themselves Christians, are still trying to win converts to Judaism instead of to Christ. Remember the letter from the Jerusalem council?"

"I remember," Mara agreed. "It was good that the apostles finally settled the issue."

Anna shook her head negatively. "In Antioch, Syria, and Cilicia, maybe, but not in Jerusalem. Christians not only have to fear the Jews who hate them, but fellow Jewish Christians as well." She shook her head again. "Persecution continues to grow there. I'm glad that I live in Samaria."

Mara became more uneasy the closer they came to their destination. If the Jews were Jehovah's chosen people, how had they come to be so lacking in compassion? Among Christians, she felt relatively safe and accepted. Among her own kind, she was afraid for her life.

A slight breeze ruffled the veils hiding her face, and Mara sighed at the coolness. She longed to throw off her coverings and walk among others unhindered as she had learned to do in Sychar. After Anna's conversation, she dared not.

Anna lifted her face slightly, her look scanning the horizon. "I hope it doesn't rain."

Mara agreed. The first rains had come early this year, and although this would be good for the planting, it would make a muddy mess of the road they were traveling. She joined Anna in searching for signs of clouds.

As they neared Jerusalem, the roads became blocked with pilgrims headed for the same destination. Travel became slow and cumbersome. Tempers flared among the crowded, pushing people.

Adonijah attached himself to Mara's side, his alert eyes watching the people around him. He sighed with relief once they were finally through the main gates and among Jerusalem's crowded streets, for though it was just as crowded here, the presence of the Roman army helped stifle angry impulses.

Barak led the way through the streets towards the Upper City where the more affluent resided. Mara noticed that he stayed as close to Anna as Adonijah did to her. She began to feel uneasy, wondering if they were expecting trouble.

The tree-lined, paved streets brought a small measure of awe to her wandering eyes. Never had she seen such large houses and yards. Even Tirinus's villa in Sychar paled in comparison.

When Barak led them down a shaded pathway to one of the larger villas, Mara finally became aware of the extent of Tirinus's wealth.

The door opened and a lady emerged, tall and thin, but with a remarkably regal bearing. She threw herself into Anna's waiting arms.

"Oh, Anna. It's so good to see you again!" She hugged Barak then, and told him, "Your mother is inside waiting in the triclinium."

Barak grinned, hurrying past her up the stairs, and disappearing inside.

The woman smiled at Mara, noting the veils with an upraised brow. Adonijah took Mara's hand and pulled her forward.

"Mara, this is Anna's Aunt Bithnia. Aunt Bithnia, my wife, Mara."

Reaching out both hands, she took Mara's cold ones into her own. Squeezing gently, she told Mara, "Welcome. You must be tired after your long trip."

Relieved by the sincere warmth of the welcome, Mara

nodded. "I am rather."

Bithnia turned to Adonijah. "Take her inside, Adonijah, and make her comfortable. Cleopas is waiting to show you to your rooms."

Adonijah grinned at the peremptory command. Bending down, he kissed Bithnia softly on her cheek. "Same old Bithnia."

She gave him a mock glare. "Old! Whom are you calling old?" Motioning with her hand, she told him, "Go on with you!"

Anna chuckled, placing one arm around her aunt's waist. Adonijah again took Mara's hand. "Come," he told her excitedly. "I want you to meet my mother."

A flood of emotions catapulted around inside of Mara, but one stood out from the others—fear. Her mouth went dry with trepidation. Adonijah looked deep into her eyes and recognized her hesitation.

"She will love you," he told her firmly. "Come."

After that, Mara could remember nothing but the warm embrace that Tamar had given her. At first Mara had been stunned by the realization that Barak's mother was a cripple, but then Tamar's lively personality helped dispel any pity Mara might have felt.

After Mara had allowed her to push aside the veils, Tamar had studied Mara's face carefully. Her gaze lingered not on the purple mark, but instead, on Mara's frightened brown eyes.

Mara was uncertain what the woman had seen there, but she had nodded her head and smiled with satisfaction. "Welcome, Daughter," she said.

Now, here she was sitting among Barak and Anna's family, an accepted part of their group. Anna had been right, both Bithnia and Tamar had welcomed her without reservation. She lifted a portion of chicken from her plate, her gaze wandering around the gathered group. There was so much joy here, it brought a lump to Mara's throat. Grandmother would have loved these people.

After supper, Barak announced that he and Adonijah would begin to build the booths. "Where do you want them?"

"In the back garden," Bithnia told him. "Cleopas will show you." After they left the room, she turned her attention to Anna and Mara. "I'm glad that you will be staying with us. Tirinus is away at present, but he hopes to be back by the end of the week."

Anna frowned at her aunt. "I hope he's not working too hard."

Shrugging, Bithnia answered her niece. "You know your father."

Anna had told Mara that her father was neither Jew nor Christian. Mara assumed that would explain his absence on this, one of the most sacred Jewish holidays; but although Bithnia was not a Jew either, she chose to celebrate the Feast of Booths with Barak and Anna.

Bithnia showed them where they would sleep for the night, since the Feast of Booths would not officially begin until tomorrow. Mara curled beneath silk sheets, their texture reminding her of her wedding night.

Would Adonijah choose to sleep with her here in Bithnia's house, or would he avoid her as he had recently started doing? The cause for his actions was beyond her understanding. All she knew was that somehow their friendship had digressed into something she couldn't describe. Sadness blended with anger, and thumping her pillow, she buried her face in its downy depths, muffling her sobs. She was asleep when Adonijah joined her.

❧

Mara forgot her troubles the next day. It was hard to be melancholy among such a boisterous, happy procession of people.

Adonijah and Barak had chosen to go to the Temple and, along with the crowd, follow the priests on their daily trek to the Spring of Gihon in the Kidron Valley. The barefoot priests and Levites were clad in white linen robes. Only the High Priest wore the breastplate of the twelve tribes, the twelve precious stones imbedded into it glowing with a rainbow of reflected color.

As the crowd walked along in the wake of the priests, they sang songs of praise and thanksgiving. Most of the crowd were waving *lulabs*, the ceremonial plumes of the woven palm, willow, and myrtle branches stirring the air around them.

The officiating priest filled a golden pitcher with water from the spring, while a chorus of Levites sang, "With joy you will draw water from the wells of salvation."

Adonijah, standing beside his wife, watched with amusement the changing expressions of her eyes as she took in the sights and sounds—awe mingled with respect, and, to a lesser extent, fear. He frowned, wishing he could rip the veil from her face and see her features more clearly.

A slight disturbance on the other side of the crowd brought his attention to bear on a large man standing opposite their party. Adonijah felt the blood drain from his face. Nudging Barak, he gestured at the older man.

Barak's eyes went wide with shock as he recognized his uncle. When the older man's baleful look rested on Anna's unsuspecting form, Barak moved closer to her side. Both he and Adonijah tensed, expecting something to happen. Instead, Uncle Simon pushed his way through the crowd and disappeared. Adonijah and Barak exchanged worried looks, and both men moved closer to their wives.

Searching intently among the people, Adonijah followed the crowd as it made its way back to the Temple. He took Mara's hand firmly within his own, trying to smile reassuringly into her questioning eyes. She could sense his unease, and the worry lines increased around her dark eyes.

When they reached the Temple, the priests marched once around the huge stone altar waving lulabs and singing, "Save us, we beseech You, O Lord, we beseech You, give us success!"

The officiating priest mounted the ramp and poured pitchers of water and wine through silver funnels onto the altar fires. Adonijah's attention was elsewhere. The dark, ominous feeling he had felt before had settled around him again.

With the ceremony ended, their party made its way back to Bithnia's house. Barak was unusually quiet, and Anna kept glancing at him trying to fathom his sudden moroseness.

Adonijah, too, had much on his mind. It was to be expected that Uncle Simon would come to Jerusalem for the Feast of Booths since it was required by Jewish law for all able-bodied Jewish males to do so, and even among such a crowd they were bound to meet.

As the sun began to set, they settled themselves among the rough shelter, their home for the next seven days. Although the top canopy of woven branches kept the sun from beating down upon them, the open sides allowed the cool afternoon breeze access.

Adonijah watched Mara and Anna preparing their meal over the open fire behind the shelter. He tried to shake himself from the dark mood he had fallen into. This was a time for feasting and celebrating. A holy time.

Barak sat down next to him. "I had hoped that over the years Uncle Simon would have mellowed, but it would seem he has not."

Adonijah nodded, his gaze resting briefly on Anna. "There was much anger in his look."

Barak sighed. "I hope he keeps his feelings to himself. Still, I am tempted to seek him out and speak with him."

Feeling his stomach churn, Adonijah raised a dark eyebrow. "Do you think that is wise?"

Barak didn't answer that question. "Tomorrow, the Apostle Peter is expected to address the assembly at the Temple after the water ceremony. I was hoping to stay and hear him."

Adonijah shifted uneasily. "Perhaps we should leave the women behind."

"My thoughts exactly."

But that was not to be the case. Anna flatly refused to be left behind the next day.

"I want to hear Peter speak," she told her husband inflexibly. When it came to matters of the spirit, and hearing God's Word, Anna could be as inflexible as the Roman war machine. Barak decided to acquiesce rather than explain his sudden misgivings. If at all possible, he would keep her from any chance meetings with his uncle.

For his part, Adonijah wondered how Uncle Simon would react to Mara. Although she *was* Jewish, she was also a Christian. Remembering Uncle Simon's reaction to Barak's and his conversions, Adonijah decided it would be best to keep Mara from his sight.

After the second day's water ceremony, when many others had departed to their temporary booth homes, Adonijah, Barak, Anna, and Mara remained behind to hear the rabbis. Tamar had volunteered to watch Ramoth and little Samah, and Bithnia had decided to stay with them.

They finally found the apostle, a large group already crowded around him. Excitedly, they settled down on the fringes of the crowd to hear him speak.

Although for some time now he had longed to hear the great man speak, Adonijah found he could not concentrate on his words. Adonijah grew tenser as time passed, his gaze continually scanning the crowd. He was concerned that Uncle Simon would suddenly appear and cause trouble for them all.

His apprehension proved to be valid when a loud, angry

voice addressed them from the edge of the crowd surrounding the apostle.

"In the days of the prophet Ezra, during the Feast of Booths, the Israeli nation was told to get rid of their foreign wives. Only then would they be acceptable to Jehovah." His shaking finger pointed at Anna. "Barak, son of Ephraim, get rid of your foreign wife."

Barak's face turned as white as the priestly tunics, then just as quickly fired red. He rose swiftly to his feet. Adonijah got to his feet as well, intent on intervening. Barak motioned him to silence, and with a voice ringing with conviction, he told his uncle, "In Christ Jesus, there is neither Jew nor Greek, slave nor free, male nor female."

Adonijah thought that it was extremely providential that the words of the Apostle Paul had come to them in a copy of a letter he had written to the churches in Galatia. They had studied the full letter in their worship assembly just this last Lord's day. Now the words took on greater meaning.

"Who is this Jesus you speak of? A false Messiah, I tell you!"

Adonijah noticed Peter standing to Barak's side. Although he remained calm, there was a zealous fire in his eyes. Before Barak could answer his uncle, Peter spoke.

"Jesus is the Christ, the Son of the living God."

After the resounding declaration, there was a momentary, eerie silence in the temple area. Then Uncle Simon's voice exploded the stillness. "Blasphemer!"

The crowd began to murmur among themselves as the confrontation continued. Before long, each man was taking sides. As voices rose in heated dispute, tempers flared among those present. Before long, the argument had escalated into a riot.

Adonijah pulled Mara to his side, wrapping his arm around her waist. "Stay close to me," he ordered tightly.

As fights erupted among those in the assembly, the din

increased. Adonijah was momentarily separated from Mara when he tried to deflect a peach hurtling towards them. In that instant, the crowd surged around them and Mara found herself pushed ever farther away from her husband.

Desperately trying to regain his side, she felt a hand grasp hers and cling. Turning with relief, she found not her husband, but Anna.

"Can you see them?" Anna yelled above the noise.

Mara shook her head. "No. Don't let go of me."

"Don't worry. I won't," Anna replied, her fingers crushing in their intensity.

Before long, Roman soldiers appeared, their helmets shining among the dusty robes of the assembled Jews. Their presence only incensed the crowd further.

One soldier bumped into Mara as he was passing. Angrily, he pushed her to the side, his eyes meeting hers briefly. He hadn't taken two steps before he whirled around to face her.

"Mara?"

It took a moment for Mara to recognize the soldier who had stopped by her house for a drink of water. She couldn't remember his name, but astonishingly, he had remembered hers. How could he possibly have recognized her behind her veils?

He came back to stand before her, his narrowed gaze focusing on her veil. "Mara?" he inquired again, trying to see past the dark barrier.

She nodded her head slightly, unable to speak. Anna glanced from one to the other, her eyes full of questions.

The soldier looked about him. Everywhere was chaos. "What are you doing here?" His lips pressed tightly together when several men shoved against them. "Come on," the soldier told her. "We have to get you out of here."

He took her by the arm, but she refused to move. "I can't. My husband—"

"Husband?" At Mara's bobbing head, he stopped. Other soldiers began swarming among the crowd, their lances poised and ready. The soldier hesitated momentarily before his face settled into tight lines of resolution. "I *have* to get you out of here now. Come with me. We'll see about your. . . your husband, later."

Not giving her time to resist, he pulled her along towards the Temple entrance. Since Anna was still clinging to Mara's fingers, she was reluctantly dragged along in their wake.

They passed through the entrance, and the soldier stopped short. As he quickly pulled them to the side, a legion of soldiers passed them going into the Temple area, their fierce, determined faces sending shivers of fear racing down Mara's back.

twelve

Trajan handed Mara a cup of water and seated himself beside her. He placed one hand on the couch behind her, leaning closer.

"It was fortunate that the gods brought us together again. I am glad that I am able to return the hospitality that you showed me," he told her softly, his eyes roaming her features.

Mara swallowed hard, shifting uneasily. Not for the first time in the past hour, she wished that Anna was still with her.

When the soldiers had arrived at the Temple, Jewish tempers, already at a high, were intensified by the arrival of the Roman guards. The angry mob had turned on the soldiers, and from what Mara could understand, several soldiers had been killed by hurtled rocks. The fact that several Jews were killed as well was of no consequence to the Roman centurion in charge. In his wrath, he had rounded up many Jews that were still in the Temple area. Adonijah and Barak had been two of those arrested.

Anna had decided to go home and inform Bithnia and Tamar of today's happenings. She hoped that her aunt might have some persuasion with the Roman authorities since Tirinus was such an important person in Jerusalem.

Mara had remained with Trajan, at his request. He had told her that he would help her reach her husband. Now, after an hour, she began to wonder. He had brought her to his villa and told her that he would send someone to get information. They were waiting for his servant to return with news.

Glancing at the soldier, Mara asked him, "Shouldn't we go and find out for ourselves what has become of my husband?

Surely those in authority would listen to you, more so than to your servant."

His slow smile sent prickles of warning dancing along Mara's skin. "My servant has gone to find out where your. . . husband is being held."

He lifted his other hand and tugged at the veil covering her face until it fell away. Gasping, Mara tried to retrieve it, but he pushed her hand away.

"Why are you hiding behind that veil?"

Honestly surprised, Mara's gaze met his. There was no revulsion in his look; only curiosity, and something else undefinable. It amazed her that he was so unaffected by her deformity.

"I thought Romans found pride in perfection," she pointed out. "Isn't it obvious why I cover my face?"

"Your people are not Roman," he told her softly, stroking a finger across her disfigurement. "Besides, no one is perfect. Is this why you hide?"

Seeing his eyes darken, Mara grew uneasy. "There was One who was perfect," she told him quietly, trying to turn his thoughts.

Something in his look made her catch her breath. She felt almost hypnotized by his intense blue eyes. He quirked an eyebrow, waiting for her to explain.

Dragging her gaze from his, she began to pull at the threads of her linen tunic. "He was the Son of God."

"Which god?"

Her lips curled into a rueful smile. "There is only one God, Trajan. The God who created us. The God who cares for us. The God who *loves* us."

He thought about what she said a moment before answering. "It must be this God that makes you so different from other women."

His voice, growing huskier by the minute, drove Mara to

her feet. She would have moved away, but quicker than she could have anticipated, he gripped her wrist and pulled her back beside him. Startled, her eyes flew to his.

"I have thought of you often," he murmured.

Mouth dropping open in surprise, she could only stare. Surely this handsome, virile Roman could have his choice of women. What he said was ludicrous, and sent her suspicions soaring. He had only met her the one time.

"It's true," he affirmed, his look once again roving over her. "There's something about you. As I said, you are different from most women I know. I want to get to know you better."

Mara tried once again to move away, but he wouldn't allow it. Her wide eyes met his. "I. . .I don't know what you are saying. I am a married woman."

His narrowed gaze watched her skeptically. The question he asked surprised her.

"Do you love your husband?"

Astonished, she gaped at him. "Of course I love my husband! Why would you ask such a question?"

"I meant no harm," he assured her soothingly, his thumb massaging her wrist. "It's just that I have heard that most Jewish marriages are arranged."

Growing more uncomfortable by the minute, she again tried to pull from his grip. His fingers held her in a gentle, but unmistakable, vise.

"Trajan," she implored, frowning with confusion. "What is it that you want from me?"

"I want *you*."

At his fervent words, Mara's insides went cold. How was this possible? She had done nothing to court his attention, had only met him once before today, and yet he wanted her. She contemplated his features, fearfully searching for some sign of insanity.

As though he could read her thoughts, he grinned. "No, I

am not a lunatic. Do you find it so incredible that a man could want you? You *are* married."

There was no way that she could explain the circumstances of her marriage to this soldier. She tried to think of something to say.

Cupping her chin in his hand, Trajan forced her eyes to meet his. "Do you *truly* love your husband?"

There was no uncertainty in her voice when she answered him. "Yes, I truly love my husband."

Disappointment flooded his face. Mara wondered if he could see the same thing in her that she had seen in Adonijah and Anna before she had become a Christian. She had longed for the peace and security they seemed to possess. Perhaps that was what Trajan saw in her and was reaching out for.

"Trajan, I want to tell you something. It's about my God."

He eyed her suspiciously, but nodded his head for her to continue. She then related everything she had been taught about salvation, and God's saving grace. When she finished, he looked confused.

"What has that to do with my desire for you?"

She gently pried his fingers from her wrist. "I think it is the love of Jesus that you *truly* desire. Not me. You only see His love in me, and you want it for yourself."

His smile was full of mockery. "You think I want to worship a *Jewish* God?"

"He is not a Jewish God. He is everyone's God."

Trajan sat back studying her, his irritation evident. "I remember now. Jewish law demands purity until marriage, and then faithfulness after."

Mara smiled affably. "While it is true that that is what Jewish law states, that is not the reason I stay with my husband. I love him, Trajan. And because I love both my husband *and* my Lord, I could never be unfaithful to either."

It was true. Before, she had wondered if what she felt for

Adonijah was love since she had never had anything to compare it with. Now, looking into this soldier's eyes, she realized that he was offering her something she no longer had any desire for. The only man she wanted attention from was her husband.

Trajan could read the sincerity in her eyes. Sighing, he slowly rose to his feet, holding out his hand. "Come. Let us go and find your Adonijah."

Hesitantly, she placed her hand in his. He lifted her to her feet until their faces were mere inches apart. For a long moment he searched her eyes, then he released her.

&.

Adonijah watched Barak trying to reason with his uncle. What streak of fate had allowed them to be placed in the same cell? Was this Jehovah's idea? He turned away, unable to watch their angry dialogue.

Leaning back against the huge block stones of the cell wall, Adonijah could feel the cold seep through his torn tunic. He was unaware of the blood slowly wending its way down the side of his head.

The darkness of the interior was relieved only by the light of a single torch. He could see others in the crowded chamber, their expressions ranging from fearful to sullen. Pulling his knees up to his chest, he wrapped his arms around them and continued his worry over Mara and Anna. Both he and Barak had tried to find out from the guards where they might be, but the soldiers refused to answer.

Were they locked up in another cell? He certainly hoped not, because the damp, dark confines of the dungeon definitely weren't meant for women. The thought of not being there to protect his wife set his teeth grinding. If anything happened to her, he would never forgive himself.

Barak dropped down beside him, his angry countenance telling its own story.

"You had no luck reaching Uncle Simon?"

"None."

Adonijah leaned his head back against the stone wall. For his part, right about now, he could care less whether Uncle Simon was reached or not. This whole thing was his fault anyway, the stubborn dolt. Closing his eyes, he began to petition Jehovah on behalf of those here in prison, and his wife and Anna as well. Barak's voice interrupted his prayers.

"If only the apostles and other disciples would write down what they remember of the Lord and His teaching. It's so hard to commit everything they say to memory. Paul's letter to the Galatians is almost being devoured by those who follow the Lord. They are hungry for any word of Him."

Adonijah agreed. "Paul says that the Spirit inspired his words. If the Spirit can inspire Paul to teach others about salvation for the Gentiles, why can't He do so with the words of Jesus? I know Philip, Paul, and Peter have taught us much of what the Lord said, but what of those in the future? How will *they* be taught? Memories grow faulty with time."

Barak sighed. "If the scriptures of Moses and the prophets were given to the Jews as God's chosen people, then He will not leave us without some word. When the time comes, the Lord will give us what we need. Right now the apostles are spread all over the Empire, and beyond, teaching others about Jesus."

Both men sat in silence, filled with their own thoughts.

Barak finally broke the silence with what was uppermost in his mind. "I hope that Anna and Mara were allowed to go home peacefully. Surely the soldiers wouldn't see them as a threat."

"I would put nothing past Roman soldiers," Adonijah disagreed. "They see us as lower than animals, women and men alike."

Again, silence fell between them. Hobnailed boots could

be heard coming their way through the passage outside. The sound stopped outside their cell. Seconds later, the door squeaked open on its iron hinges.

A soldier moved into the room, his torch lifted above his head to push back the darkness. Peering through squinted eyes, his look ranged the dark confines around him.

"Which of you is Adonijah?" he barked.

Adonijah came swiftly to his feet, Barak beside him.

"I am."

The guard moved the torch until he could see Adonijah's standing figure. "Come out. And the one called Barak as well."

Adonijah and Barak exchanged glances. They slowly made their way towards where the guard stood glowering at them.

Once outside, the guard led them down the dimly lit passageway past other cells until they reached the landing above. Taking out a key, the guard opened a huge iron door and motioned the two men inside.

"Wait here," he told them.

Reluctantly, Adonijah and Barak did as they were told.

"What do you think is going on?" Adonijah asked, seating himself on a stone bench. The only other furniture in the room was a large wooden table that contained the remains of some earlier meal.

Barak continued to stand. "I don't know. Maybe Bithnia was able to convince the authorities that we are no threat."

Before long, the guard returned with another Roman soldier. He glanced first at Barak, then at Adonijah. His eyes widened with recognition.

"You! You are the one called Adonijah?"

Adonijah recognized the soldier from the road, the one who had spoken to him about Mara. He got slowly to his feet.

"I am."

One arrogant eyebrow lifted upwards. "I might have known it would be you," he told Adonijah obliquely. "Both of you come with me."

They followed him through passages, ever upward. Finally, they came out into a large antechamber. There was a Roman tribune sitting at a small table. He leaned back in his chair, tapping a pen stylus against his lips, watching as they crossed to stand before him.

He glanced at the young soldier. "These are the two you spoke of, Trajan?"

Trajan snapped a salute. "Yes, Tribune."

The tribune's look once again fastened on the two men standing before him. "You are family to one Tirinus of Sychar?"

Surprised, Adonijah and Barak nodded. Had Anna's aunt then been able to persuade the authorities to let them go?

The tribune laid down the stylus. "I know of Tirinus. He is a good man, not one to cause trouble." The look he gave them told them exactly what he thought of *them*. "Trajan tells me that you weren't involved in the riot. Is this so?"

Before Adonijah could open his mouth, Barak answered. "No, that is not so."

The tribune's eyebrows lifted upwards, his angry look fixing on Trajan. The young soldier kept his eyes on the far wall without responding. The tribune's look came back to Barak.

"So. You were involved then?"

Barak sighed. "My uncle and I had a small dispute, and others took sides. Before I knew what was happening, a riot ensued."

Lifting the stylus from the table again, the tribune began to twist it in his fingers without glancing up. "And this. . . dispute. Did it have anything to do with Roman authority?"

"No, Tribune," Barak answered honestly. "It was a religious matter."

Frowning, the tribune got to his feet. Circling to stand behind them, he said, "Ever fighting over religion. You Jews are an intolerant people."

Both Adonijah and Barak refrained from comment. The tribune came to stand before them again until he could look them squarely in the eye. "Did you hurl rocks at the Roman guards?"

"No, Tribune," Barak answered.

"And you?" he inquired of Adonijah.

"No, Tribune."

The tribune leaned back on his palms against the table, crossing his feet at the ankles. "Since I have no proof otherwise, and I have Trajan's word that it was neither of you who did kill my soldiers, you may leave." His eyes became fierce. "But let me make myself clear. If I *ever* have trouble with either of you again, I will not be so lenient."

"What of the others?" Adonijah wanted to know.

Lifting his head, the tribune's fathomless eyes met Adonijah's. "You may leave. . .*now*."

Both Adonijah and Barak wanted to argue, but they resisted. It would do no one any good to anger the tribune further.

Adonijah stepped forward and chanced one last question. "Were there any women arrested?"

The tribune glanced at Trajan. The soldier snapped to attention, answering his superior's unasked question. "There were a few, Tribune, but not the ones they seek."

Adonijah's surprised look focused on the young soldier. Trajan gave him a warning look. Puzzled, Adonijah silently followed the soldier from the room. Barak, who hadn't missed the look, was close on his heels.

Opening the door to the outside, they flinched as their eyes tried to adjust to the waning sunlight. Trajan turned to Barak. "You may leave. Your wife is at home waiting for you. You," he pointed to Adonijah, "come with me."

Barak questioned Adonijah with his eyes. "You go ahead," Adonijah told him. "Make sure Anna is well. I will be along later."

"Are you certain?" Barak asked, his suspicious look settling on the young Roman.

Adonijah nodded, watching as his friend unwillingly took his departure. Turning, he fell into step behind Trajan. "Where are we going?"

"To my villa. Mara is waiting for you there."

Adonijah's simmering suspicions suddenly boiled into churning certainty. Hands clenching into fists at his side, he opened his mouth to ask a barrage of questions, only to have them checked by Trajan's one insolent question.

"Do you love your wife?"

There was something in the soldier's voice that Adonijah couldn't quite put a name to. Urgency? Desperation? He stopped, but Trajan never checked his stride. Adonijah had to hurry to catch up with him. "Why do you ask such a thing?"

Trajan glanced at him briefly. "Just curious. I know that Jews often arrange marriages, and I wondered if yours was such a one."

"Nobody arranged our marriage except Mara and myself," he told Trajan flatly.

"Then you do love her?"

They passed several buildings before Adonijah finally answered. "Not that it's any concern of yours, but, yes, I love my wife."

Trajan stopped before a white concrete wall that led to a small villa. He pushed open the gate, and motioned Adonijah inside. Closing the gate behind him, Trajan smiled wryly at Adonijah. Pursing his lips, he told Adonijah, "I had hoped for a different answer."

"How long have you known my wife?" Adonijah demanded.

The Roman lifted one dark brow disdainfully. "Don't get hostile with me. I met your wife only once before today. Having met her only once, I still knew that she was a special woman. I have learned in my life, and *especially* in my occupation, never to let an opportunity pass. A woman such as Mara is extremely rare."

Adonijah couldn't agree more, but hearing this Roman say so made his blood boil. Jealousy warred with admiration. "You must be a special man to be able to see that," he told the soldier reluctantly.

Surprised, Trajan contemplated Adonijah, one hand resting on the handle to his door. His lips twisted slightly. "You mean because of the mark on her face?" He snorted softly. "Let's just say that I have had a lot of experience with human nature. One so gentle and loving stands out quite clearly in this sordid world." His eyes narrowed. "Some of the finest men *and* women that I have ever known were not much to look at."

Adonijah said nothing.

"I didn't know that Mara was married, though truth to tell, it wouldn't have mattered."

Opening the door, he allowed Adonijah to precede him through it. Motioning to a door off to their left, he stood back. "In there. I'll return in a moment to say good-bye." Turning, he strode from sight.

Adonijah hesitated before entering the room. It was obvious that the young soldier was smitten with his wife. Could she tell? Would it make a difference to her, knowing it? He had known for some time now that his own feelings for his wife were growing—evolving into something more complex than he had ever suspected. But did she feel the same way about him? For a time he had believed so, but lately. . .

He found her staring out the window to the garden beyond. "Mara," he called softly.

She turned at his voice. Her face lit with joy, and Adonijah felt his heart give a mighty lurch. Surely she wouldn't look so pleased to see him if she didn't have some feelings for him.

"Adonijah!" Swiftly she crossed the room to his side. She paused, uncertain of her reception. He reached out and pulled her into his arms.

"Thank Jehovah you are all right," he told her, holding her close against his body. He held her within the shelter of his arms, and for a moment, neither was able to speak. Lifting her face from his chest, Mara examined his eyes.

"Praise Jehovah that *you* are all right," she responded, relieved to have him near once more. "What of Barak?"

"Barak is even now on his way home to Anna."

Mara once more laid her head on his chest, content to be together after such a frightening experience. Adonijah's hands moved in comforting circles across her back. At her soft murmur, she felt his heart increase its rhythm beneath her cheek.

Adonijah took a deep breath. For a long while now, this was exactly what he had wanted to do. Still, he had to give Mara the opportunity she deserved. She had always thought herself unloved, and therefore she had accepted his offer of marriage. Was it possible that she might have reciprocating feelings for the soldier, Trajan? Despite the fact that he was a Roman, Adonijah found himself unable to dislike the man.

"Mara," he began, unable to let go of her and look her in the face. He didn't know if he could bear to have her leave him. In his heart, he knew that she would never turn from her vows, but what were vows without love? "The soldier, Trajan, has feelings for you."

Mara pulled back from his hold, looking into his eyes. She could see the pain in their amber depths. "I have feelings for no one but you," she told him softly.

He continued to study her, his eyes darkening until she could see nothing but her own reflection within. "Are you absolutely certain?" he demanded. His fingers closed over her shoulders, pushing her slightly away. "Mara, you must be positive, because once you say you belong to me, I will never let you go."

She placed her hands on his forearms. "I am certain, Adonijah. And you?"

He pulled her close again, both arms wrapped securely around her. He buried his face in her neck. "I love you," he told her huskily. "I think I must have from the very beginning."

Lifting his head, he stroked a thumb across her bottom lip. His gaze held hers as their eyes flashed messages of mutual love. Groaning softly, he covered her lips with his own.

Wrapping her arms around his neck, Mara closed her eyes tightly. A lone tear managed to squeeze through her closed lids, running silently down her cheek. *Oh, Lord Jesus,* she thought. *Thank You! Thank You for Your bountiful blessings!* If there had been any doubts in her mind about Jehovah's will for her life, they were decisively put to rest.

The door opened, making them jerk apart. Trajan peered inside, one eyebrow quirked upwards. "Ready to go?" he asked, noting Mara's flushed countenance.

Adonijah glanced at him briefly before returning his loving gaze to his wife. Finally, they could go home and face the future together. Yes, they were ready for whatever came their way. "Ready."

Taking his wife by the hand, Adonijah nodded to Trajan as they passed. It was odd how Jehovah had used this Roman to help Mara and himself realize their feelings for each other.

Trajan stood on the steps watching them until they were at the gate. Adonijah turned back to him, smiling slowly. "You're not exactly what I thought an angel would look like."

"Angel?" Perplexed, the soldier stared at him.

Adonijah grinned. "Someday, I think you just might understand. I'll. . ." He stopped, his look resting on Mara. "*We* will pray for you," he finished softly.

Mara nodded, glancing at Trajan. Her smile lit her face until one hardly noticed the deformity. "Jehovah be with you, Trajan. Thank you for your lovely compliment, but remember what I said."

Trajan watched them leave, shaking his head in wonder. Angels? Gods? He didn't understand any of it. He wasn't certain that he really wanted to. Still, there was something about them that set his heart yearning. Perhaps it was his infatuation with the woman, or perhaps it was just his envy of what Adonijah possessed.

No, he didn't understand any of it, but didn't Mara say that a man named Peter did? And wasn't that man still in prison for today's riot? Perhaps this man that Mara called an apostle could explain a few things to him, like what caused such peace to reside in Mara's lovely, dark eyes. He had longed for such peace for some time now, and not just the peace of the Pax Romana. No, Roman peace hadn't warmed the coldness in his soul. His gaze wandered towards the Antonia, the fortress where prisoners were being held. Biting his lip, he headed in that direction.

A Letter To Our Readers

Dear Reader:

In order that we might better contribute to your reading enjoyment, we would appreciate your taking a few minutes to respond to the following questions. We welcome your comments and read each form and letter we receive. When completed, please return to the following:

Rebecca Germany, Fiction Editor
Heartsong Presents
PO Box 719
Uhrichsville, Ohio 44683

1. Did you enjoy reading *Mark of Cain?*
   ☐ Very much. I would like to see more books
      by this author!
   ☐ Moderately
      I would have enjoyed it more if _____

   _____

   _____

2. Are you a member of **Heartsong Presents**? Yes ☐ No ☐
   If no, where did you purchase this book?_____

   _____

3. How would you rate, on a scale from 1 (poor) to 5 (superior),
   the cover design?_____

4. On a scale from 1 (poor) to 10 (superior), please rate the
   following elements.

   _____ Heroine   _____ Plot

   _____ Hero   _____ Inspirational theme

   _____ Setting   _____ Secondary characters

5. These characters were special because _____

_____

_____

6. How has this book inspired your life? _____

_____

_____

7. What settings would you like to see covered in future
   Heartsong Presents books? _____

_____

_____

8. What are some inspirational themes you would like to see
   treated in future books? _____

_____

_____

9. Would you be interested in reading other **Heartsong
   Presents** titles?   Yes ❏   No ❏

10. Please check your age range:
    ❏ Under 18   ❏ 18-24   ❏ 25-34
    ❏ 35-45   ❏ 46-55   ❏ Over 55

11. How many hours per week do you read? _____

Name _____

Occupation _____

Address _____

City _____ State _____ Zip _____

Travel along

with those brave adventurers who
dared to make their homes from the
untamed frontiers of America's west.
Colleen L. Reece uses years of
research and writing experience to
bring to life four complete novels of
historical inspirational romance. In
Flower of Seattle, Brian O'Rourke
embarks on a journey from devastated
Ireland to the Seattle Territory where
love will surprise him in the form of a

Scottish blossom of womanhood. Their daughter Daisy is
drawn in *Flower of the West* to the Arizona Territory to serve as
a Harvey Girl, mature into a godly woman, and befriend a
mysterious cowboy. Search for peace and purpose leads
Bernard Clifton to the harsh frontier of Alaska in *Flower of the
North*, but he may not feel worthy of a true love. Then, in *Flower
of Alaska*, Arthur Baldwin has unfinished business which will
lead him to Alaska, but the love of his life doesn't want to let
him go into the harsh, untamed frontier.

paperback, 464 pages, 5 ⅞" x 8"

❤ ❤ ❤ ❤ ❤ ❤ ❤ ❤ ❤ ❤ ❤ ❤ ❤ ❤ ❤ ❤

Please send me _____ copies of *Frontiers*. I am enclosing $4.97 for each.
Please add $1.00 to cover postage and handling per order. OH add 6% tax.)
Send check or money order, no cash or C.O.D.s please.

Name_____

Address _____

City, State, Zip _____

To place a credit card order, call 1-800-847-8270.
Send to: Heartsong Presents Reader Service, PO Box 719, Uhrichsville, OH 44683

❤ ❤ ❤ ❤ ❤ ❤ ❤ ❤ ❤ ❤ ❤ ❤ ❤ ❤ ❤ ❤

·····Heart♥ng·····

HISTORICAL ROMANCE IS CHEAPER BY THE DOZEN!

Any 12 *Heartsong Presents* titles for only $26.95 *

Buy any assortment of twelve *Heartsong Presents* titles and save 25% off of the already discounted price of $2.95 each!

*plus $1.00 shipping and handling per order and sales tax where applicable.

HEARTSONG PRESENTS TITLES AVAILABLE NOW:

(If ordering from this page, please remember to include it with the order form.)